THE *ex* FILES SERIES

EXCHANGE

LISA RYAN CAMPBELL

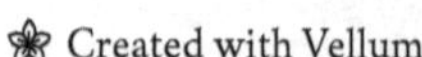 Created with Vellum

For Mom,

Thank you for giving me life. I'm eternally grateful for you.

One year earlier...

The Superior Court lay nestled in the heart of Civic Center in downtown San Francisco. Outside, rang the busy sounds of locals making their way to work, mingling with tourists who traveled to the city by the thousands to see its sights. But inside the courthouse, in a packed room, not a sound was heard as Vanessa Johnson gave a shocking and teary-eyed confession of her ongoing affair with her arresting officer.

"I never meant for this to happen." She paused and looked to Sergeant Jason Arnold, who sat behind the prosecutor's desk. "*We* never meant for this to happen."

Although his expression was unreadable, she knew he was seething inside. He never wanted the truth about their affair to come out. He even begged her to keep quiet when he met her at some shady bar in the Bernal Heights district where neither of them was known too well.

"You're going to fuck up my career, my marriage, everything," he hissed above the music and conversation around them.

"I'm not going to prison," she said. "I've been on the stand for

two days now, and that bitch is raking me over the coals. The jury is ready to send me away." She took a sip of the drink he'd ordered for her. "This is my only choice now, since you didn't do your job and make this case go away."

"That wasn't my fault. My partner was like a dog with a bone. He was determined to nail your ass. That's why I told you to leave town in the first place."

"And go where? Do what? Hide for the rest of my life?"

"I would've come for you. We could've started a life somewhere else."

She gave him a look that said she knew he was feeding her bullshit. Jason Arnold wasn't going anywhere. He was on track to become lieutenant, and his wife was the new rising star at the district attorney's office. He said she was even offered a job as a litigator at some prestigious law firm. They were San Francisco's next power couple, and she'd be a fool to think he'd give any of that up. When it came down to it, Jason Arnold was going to take care of himself, and she needed to do the same.

Vanessa had been out on bond for four months leading up to her trial and had moved in with her mother for the time being. Staying home with Carl was completely out of the question. As the weeks passed, whenever she saw him, she felt a chill go up her spine. He knew what she'd done, and he wanted her dead.

Now, as he sat in the last row of the courtroom, she refused to make eye contact with him as she told everyone that she and Jason had been having an affair long before she was arrested for murder. Yes, her reputation as a woman would suffer. No doubt, the trolls were already online calling her every vile name in the book for not just allegedly killing her stepson, but for sleeping with a married man. She would be labeled a whore for the rest of her life. But at least she'd be a free whore.

"When he put the handcuffs on me, my heart broke," she

said, sobbing and giving as good a performance as she could while everyone stayed riveted in their seats by the drama being played out before them. "I knew it hurt him too, but he was doing his duty."

As an added effect, she dared to look his wife in the eye and added, "We never meant to hurt anyone."

The moment her attorney ended his questioning, the courtroom broke out in an uproar with the sensational case now erupted. Judge Walter Matson banged his gavel several times to bring order, but this was too much for everyone to digest at once.

"This court will take a brief recess," he said over the continued rumble of conversation. "Counselors, I want you both in my chambers."

Vanessa smiled inwardly. She wasn't going to prison today. As the bailiff escorted her from the stand, she looked to Jason, who was in a heated conversation with his partner. After a moment, they both left the courtroom, still arguing in hushed tones and pushing reporters out of their way, who were clamoring for comment. She always thought the other one was much more handsome than Jason, but too bad he wouldn't leave it alone. He wanted to see her hang for her alleged crimes, and coupled with Jason's ADA wife, Vanessa was left without options. So, she told her attorney the story and gave him the ammunition needed to bring this case to a halt.

As she was being led back to the holding facility, she chanced a look to the back of the courtroom and saw that Carl remained sitting completely still, and his expression had not changed as he boldly returned her stare. She quickly looked away, feeling that familiar chill again. For the first time, she began considering Jason's suggestion to leave town.

* * *

Judge Walter Matson's decision was final. He'd met the two opposing counselors in chambers only to inform them of his planned ruling, and the young, vibrant ADA made it her duty to let him know just how much pain this would cause the Johnson family. But he remained firm in his stance. As he reminded the prosecutor, this case had turned into a circus, namely because one of her investigating officers had aired his dirty laundry for all the world to see, and in effect, made his courtroom a laughing stock.

"This is more than just a technicality," he said. "They were sleeping together, for Christ's sake!"

"You know she's guilty, your honor," the young woman continued doggedly. "You cannot let her walk out of here."

"Watch your tone, counselor. You know I have no choice in this matter."

She did back down then, and Matson felt guilt wash over him. She must be feeling so humiliated. He looked to her opponent and saw the gleam in his eyes. He'd been all but itching to get back to the courtroom and claim a victory. And now, his moment had come.

Matson faced the prosecutor again and softened his tone. "I know he's your husband, and this must be hard for you to deal with right now—"

Her eyes flashed with repressed anger. "That has nothing to do with it. Whether she and my husband carried on an affair doesn't negate the fact that she's guilty and that you're about to let a murderess go free."

Matson sighed, giving up the battle, and rose from his seat behind his desk. "I'm sorry, Mrs. Arnold, but my decision has been made."

Back in his courtroom, he made his announcement with regret. "Ladies and gentlemen of the jury. I appreciate your patience as the Court took the time to decide what to do with this new revelation. I have spoken with counsels on my position, and due to an extreme conflict of interest between the defendant and an officer of the San Francisco police department, I am hereby declaring a mistrial."

He banged the gavel with finality. "Court is adjourned. The jury is dismissed. Mrs. Johnson, you are free to go."

The chatter began with full force as reporters dictated into their recorders and made calls about the turn of events. As Judge Matson rose, he caught a glimpse of the ADA grabbing her things and pushing her way through the crowd. One of the officers scheduled to testify made a grab for her arm, but she yanked it free, giving him a look that chilled the blood even in the Judge's veins. Mentally shaking his head, he gathered his legal pad and pen and headed for chambers, trying not to look into the eyes of Mr. Johnson.

But he couldn't help sparing the man a glance, and what he saw stopped him. There wasn't just pain, but utter helplessness. While his wife cried over relief and happiness that she'd escaped a murder conviction, Carl Johnson simply watched her. And in that moment, Judge Matson was afraid for her.

CHAPTER ONE

*P*resent day…
"You're playing a dangerous game."

"Am I?"

He stepped closer to her with menace laced in his eyes. "Trust me, Angela. You're going to regret going down this road."

She cocked her head to one side. "Are you threatening me?"

"That's a promise."

She laughed. "You don't get it do you? This isn't just about you. This story, this whole fucking mess is one year in the making."

Angela paced back and forth in the living area of the suite she'd rented for the night, still seething from the conversation she'd just had a half an hour ago. She'd been waiting for Sophie to show but instead, she got an uninvited guest. No one was supposed to know she was staying here, except Sophie, but he'd found her, barged in with accusations and… Angela frowned to herself. The things he'd said to her—they didn't make any sense.

As she continued to pace the small area back and forth, she did her best to try to get the pieces of his conversation to fit. But the only way she could see the puzzle form meant that something else was going on that she had never been aware of. Something like deception. She came to a stop just as realization struck her.

"Oh, Sophie," she said softly to herself. "What have you done?"

A notification sound came from her cell, indicating she had a text. She dug it out of her purse and read the text from her sister.

Work ran late. I have a few more papers to file and I'll be there.

Angela, feeling herself fill with anger, sent a quick text back to Sophie and then shoved the phone back into her purse. She was confident that when her sister read those words, it would get her here a lot quicker, desperate to explain what she'd done. She hoped the damage wasn't so catastrophic that it ruined her story. Even though, this wasn't just some story.

What she would take to her editor Monday morning had the power to destroy someone's life. Yes, she was bringing down one of San Francisco's finest, but when they found out this fellow officer was involved in murder and the further cover up of that murder, they would be thanking her for her service.

She had to keep reminding herself this was all justified. She and so many cops of the SFPD had been played for fools from the very beginning, and she was anxious for Sophie to get here so she could tell her everything.

As if on auto pilot, she made her way to the bathroom and looked longingly toward the bathtub. After her visitor, the realization of what Sophie had done, and the anticipation of the shitstorm that her finished story would cause, her nerves were completely shot and a headache was slowly brewing. She glanced down at her watch, mentally calculated the time it would take before Sophie arrived, and then looked to the bathtub again. Without any more thought, she turned on the hot water faucet and jets and poured bubble bath soap into the tub.

While the tub filled with water, Angela picked at the wilting salad she'd ordered earlier from room service and tried to bite back the sinking feeling that something was terribly wrong. She'd done her research, she had corroborating witnesses, and most important of all, she had her source, who was now suddenly MIA. But what it all boiled down to was she had Jason's killer.

She turned off the running water, undressed, and slowly dipped her feet in before submerging her entire body. A blissful sigh escaped her lips as the massaging jets and warmth of the water surrounding her made her feel safe. Moments later, she heard the faint sound of the room door opening and closing. The click of the room key and the sound of the door being opened startled her at first, and then she let out a relieved sigh. Sophie was finally here. She'd been sure to leave a key with the concierge in her sister's name to avoid any delays.

"I'm in the bathtub," she called out. "Give me a minute."

She could hear her sister's footsteps along the carpeted floor as she made her way to the bathroom. Angela's back was to the open door, so she didn't see her when she came in, stood behind her, and simply watched.

Angela sighed and spoke without turning around. "Listen, you're the one who is late, so just give me a minute. We can talk about everything when I get out, including Ethan."

But there came no reply, and Angela felt instinctively that the atmosphere in the room had changed. Despite the hot water, she suddenly felt cold and vulnerable. She turned her body partially, saw who it was, and cried out just as strong hands came around her throat and plunged her body under the soapy water.

CHAPTER TWO

*A*nita grabbed for her purse and carryon suitcase. She had one hour to make an evening flight to Portland and be with her daughter who was going into labor. Just as she was about to turn the light off in her office, her desk phone rang.

"Damn," she said.

Normally, she wouldn't have answered it, but her boss liked to make infrequent phone calls at night to reassure himself that things were still running smoothly.

"Thank you for calling Franklin Hotel. This is Anita Sykes; how may I help you?"

Silence followed.

"Hello?"

"I need a favor."

She immediately recognized the voice, dropped her purse, and sat in her desk chair. "I have a plane to catch in an hour. Are you sure this can't wait?"

"I wouldn't have bothered if it could. I don't have time to explain over the phone. I can meet you at the airport, but I need you to bring something with you."

Anita picked up her cell phone and checked the time. "I'll be at San Francisco International in twenty minutes. What do you need from me?"

* * *

Two hours later…

The cell phone vibrated across the wooden coffee table where Ethan's feet rested. He glanced away from the baseball game on TV and looked down at the display.

Angela, it read.

He tipped the bottle of beer he'd been holding in one hand to his mouth, took a lazy sip, and returned his eyes to the game—but his attention had already been broken. That was twice she'd called in five minutes, which wasn't like her. She didn't hound someone constantly with calls. One call with no answer, and she hung up. If it was important, she would've left a voicemail or simply sent him a text.

Ethan dropped his feet to the floor and leaned forward, bracing his elbows on his knees. He stared at the indicator on the phone, letting him know he now had two missed calls but no waiting voice mail or text. Curiosity got the better of him, and he was interested to hear just what she had to say for herself after he accused her of trying to ruin his career and damage his reputation. He really didn't have proof of any of that, but he had rumors and conjectures, and like it or not, the workplace grapevine was sometimes the best source for the truth. What he couldn't understand was how she could convince him to take her in his confidence only to turn his secrets against him. All those evenings he'd met her for dinner or drinks or the calls in which he had opened up to her had been therapeutic for him. He had a lot he needed to get off his chest, and she'd been the perfect sounding board, just like always. But it was clear she'd been using him to get answers, and he was left looking like a fool.

The phone vibrated again. It was her. Ethan, now pissed all over again, snatched it up.

"Yeah," he answered, ready to lay into her.

"Ethan, come quick. She's dead. I—I didn't touch her."

He stood up, the stress in her voice immediately snapping to attention. "Slow down, breathe and tell me what's going on."

"There's no time for that! I'm at Franklin Hotel. I should have called 9-1-1, but you're the first person I could think of."

"Stay where you are. I'll be there." He was heading to the front door, grabbing his badge and gun along the way.

"Ethan?"

"Yeah?"

"They killed her. Somebody killed her."

"Angie, just stay where you are. I'm coming now."

There was a long silence, and Ethan thought she hung up when he heard a sigh.

"Wrong girl, Ethan. This is Sophie."

Ethan came to a full stop, took the phone from his ear, and stared at the caller ID display again and frowned. "Sophie?"

The line went dead.

CHAPTER THREE

*E*than arrived at the hotel in less than twenty minutes, parked his vehicle in an illegal spot, and raced through the lobby, flashing his badge to the confused-looking concierge.

Angela was dead. Angela was dead?

He'd been talking to Sophie and those had been her words. Someone killed her. But what was Sophie doing here at Franklin Hotel? Were they supposed to meet here? Had Angela called her sister? Was the murderer still on the premises?

A thousand more questions raced through Ethan's mind as he punched the elevator button over and over again, staring up at the numbers as they slowly lit their descent floor by floor until finally reaching the lobby. He punched the button for the seventh floor and cursed himself as the doors closed slowly. He'd ignored her calls, thinking it was Angela who had been calling, when the whole time it was Sophie, calling from Angela's phone and needing his help.

The elevator doors chimed open, and he practically ran

through the corridor, glancing at the brass numbers of each room he passed.

716…718…720…722.

He rapped on the door in quick succession. "This is the police. Open the door."

When the door remained closed, he removed his gun from his waistband, pulled his sleeve over his hand, and tried the door handle. Locked. He hadn't stopped to grab a key card from the front desk, because he was sure Sophie would be there to let him inside the room. He looked up and down the hall, hoping to find a maid to let him in. He didn't want to have to go all the way back down to the lobby and talk to the front desk clerk, but that might be his only solution. Where the hell was Sophie?

Then, almost indistinctly, he heard movement from inside the room, and then something crashed to the floor. Ethan raised his gun with one hand and pounded on the door with the other.

"Sophie! Are you in there? Open the door!"

More movement from inside, but it wasn't sounds of struggle. It sounded like she was looking for something.

He pounded harder this time. "Open the door now!"

From behind him, another room door opened, and a sleepy-eyed man stepped out. "What the hell is all the noise for? I've got a meeting in the morning, so take it somewhere else."

"I'm a cop, sir. Get back in your room, now," Ethan commanded.

Coupled with the tone of his voice and the big black gun he was holding, the man inched back and closed the door, not before muttering "I'm calling the manager."

Ethan turned back to room 722 and was about to issue a warning for whoever was inside to stand back, when the door swung open and Sophie came stumbling out, looking as if she were running from the devil.

"Ethan! I… I…"

She bent to the waist and vomited on the floor.

He touched her back. "Where is she?"

She wiped her mouth and looked up at him with fear in her eyes and her brown skin turning pale. "I… I didn't do it. I swear I didn't touch her."

Ethan put one foot in the door to keep it from shutting and sat her down along the wall.

"Keep your head between your legs and don't move."

He moved inside the hotel room with his gun drawn and tried to not be distracted by the fact that the place was a mess. Furniture was turned over, drawers flung open, and what looked to be the contents of Angela's purse had been dumped out onto the floor. There was no one in the immediate sitting room or the bedroom. He kept moving toward the bathroom, being led by the smell of bath salts…and death.

He came to the entrance to the bathroom and stopped just at the threshold. The body lay in the tub with one arm extended over the rim and the other over her head. Water was everywhere, indicating she'd fought and fought hard before being beaten by the water burning in her lungs.

He moved inside, careful not to disturb anything, until he was standing beside the tub, and she was in full view of him. The same identical face, now blue from asphyxiation and the same deep brown eyes as the woman he'd left in the hall now stared sightless up at the ceiling.

Ethan regarded the woman who'd been a pest to him as a girl, a confidante to him as a young woman, and ultimately the would-be nail in his coffin and lowered his head in sadness and regret. He then turned away and stepped back out into the living area where he pulled out his cell and called for backup.

CHAPTER FOUR

Sixteen months earlier (Four months before the trial)…

"I've wanted you to meet him for a long time. He was just transferred from missing persons to homicide."

"It's been a while since you had a partner." Sophie took a sip of her wine, and surreptitiously glanced at her watch, silently willing this new partner of Jason's to enter the restaurant now so they could have their dinner, and she could return to the office to begin prepping for this new case.

"I'll warn you. He's trying to prove himself with the Johnson case. He gained a good reputation in missing persons, and my Lieutenant was more than happy to hand him the case right off the bat."

"The Lieutenant trusts you, too," Sophie said, not wanting Jason to sell himself short.

"Yeah, but I probably wouldn't have got the case if I didn't have a partner. This happened at the right time," he said, grinning at her. "I'll try to keep the dinner friendly, but he's eager to get started, so don't be surprised if he wants to talk to you about your progress."

"I can take care of myself," she said, smiling and taking another sip of wine.

When her supervisor brought her the new case file a few days ago, she admitted to herself, she'd been annoyed. She was cleaning out her office and closing out all cases in preparation for her new position at Becker and Reynolds, and the last thing she needed was to have more work dropped in her lap. But when he explained what the case was about, something inside of her stirred. The defendant, Vanessa Johnson, was accused of slowly poisoning her stepson. The motive being she didn't want the competition for her new husband's time and attention. She was pleading innocent, with her lawyer claiming the boy had always been sickly. Sophie received the discovery file in which the defense attorney managed to subpoena the boy's medical records, which only supported Vanessa Johnson's claims that her stepson died of natural causes. But Sophie suspected something deeper was going on and wanted justice for the little boy and his father. She would be working with her husband, Jason, and his new partner. As a prosecutor, she frequently worked with the arresting officers on a case, but this had the potential of being a sensational trial. The media wouldn't be able to resist, and she wasn't ashamed to admit that she was excited to show San Francisco just how much of a good team she and Jason were together.

"Here he is." Jason rose from the table with a wide smile to shake his new partner's hand. When Sophie met the man's face, she was slower to stand to her feet as the two men turned toward her and Jason made the introductions.

"Sophie, this is Ethan Markham. Ethan, my wife, Sophia."

They simply smiled at each other, and Ethan, albeit

slowly, was the first to reach out his hand toward her. She took it in hers and grasped it.

"You can call me Sophie."

"It's good to meet you, finally," Ethan said, gesturing for her to return to her seat. "Jason talks about you, a lot. I hear you're going to be trying the Johnson case."

"That's right," she said, unable to stop looking at him. There were the same striking gray eyes, firm cheekbones and hard jawline. The young and carefree boy she'd known had given way to a mature, handsome man.

"So, are you in or out?" Ethan's tone and easy demeanor suddenly changed, and the pasted smile she'd been wearing disappeared.

"Excuse me?"

"I came by your office a few days ago to talk to you about the case. Your assistant said you were out, but I was there long enough to see all the boxes. I couldn't tell whether you were moving in or out of there."

"I'm moving out, actually. Technically, I still work for the DA's office, but as it happens, the Johnson case will be my last for this office."

"On to bigger and better things?"

She gave him a wan smile. "Something like that."

"She's being modest," Jason said, taking her hand. "Sophie has been offered a position as a junior litigator for Becker and Reynolds." Jason paused to wink at Ethan. "Very prestigious."

She didn't miss the look Ethan gave their intertwined hands. There was something hard in his gaze, but it gradually faded away as he raised his eyes to meet hers. "Congratulations. Are you in or out?"

"Easy partner," Jason said.

"It's okay," she interjected and then addressed Ethan. "I know this is a serious case, but I only just received the discovery file and haven't had a chance to prepare my prosecution."

"I hear you're good, so I shouldn't have to tell you I need your focus on this one."

"Are you telling me how to do my job?"

He leaned forward and rested his arms on the table. "I'm telling you I need you focused. Your cushy new job will be there when this case is done."

"Well, thank you, Sergeant, but I don't need your confidence in me. I also don't need you to tell me what cases are serious, because frankly, they're all serious to me, which is why I'm good and being offered the cushy new job."

She and Ethan seemed to embark on a staring contest that managed to suck the energy from the room. Suddenly, she felt as though it were only the two of them in the restaurant.

"Give me the overview," she said.

"Wait, this is supposed to be a friendly dinner," Jason complained. "No shop talk."

"All three of us will be on this case together. There's no better time than now to start preparing," Ethan said.

Jason looked to Ethan and then Sophie, and must have seen the determination in both of their eyes. He leaned back in his seat with his drink in one hand and waved his other hand, indicating for Ethan to proceed to give her the facts about the case.

"Eight-year-old Matthew Johnson was pronounced dead by his primary physician due to a chronic illness he suffered from. But after his death, his father, Dr. Carl Johnson, used his pull with the medical examiner's office to have his son's body autopsied as soon as possible."

"What pull?" she asked.

He's the assistant M.E."

She nodded and indicated for him to continue.

"Traces of the drug Trisenox were found in the boy's body, which carry small doses of arsenic. Not too much to do harm, but when given in frequent doses over time to a boy with an already weakened immune system, it could cause some internal damage and prove fatal. Vanessa Johnson is a pharmacist and has access to the drug. Jason and I questioned Carl Johnson and found that Vanessa was the one in charge of preparing Matthew's meals. The two had a nanny due to their busy schedules, but Vanessa made it a point to serve the boy his breakfast, pack his lunch for school, and be home in time to make dinner."

"You subpoenaed the records from the pharmacy she works for?"

He nodded. "A large amount of Trisenox was ordered in the last six months before the boy's death. The pharmacy technicians that work under Johnson say that kind of order is unusual for one pharmacy, but they didn't question it because she was the senior pharmacist."

"I'm hearing the motive is jealousy."

Jason spoke up this time. "That's what we're going with. Along with the hours Dr. Johnson works, his son's illness consumes a lot of his time. From what I've heard about Vanessa, she's a woman who craves being the center of attention. She is his second wife and does not have any children of her own. We have witnesses who will testify that Vanessa repeatedly expressed anger at having to play second fiddle to his ailing son."

"Where's the boy's biological mother?" she asked.

"Dr. Johnson tells me his ex-wife, Laura, and he no longer speak," Ethan said. "He says she never wanted the boy and he gave her a divorce in exchange for full custody. He says she came by to visit one day, after being MIA for six years. He didn't want Matthew to be confused by the sight of a new face, so he gave his wife some pictures and asked her to never visit again."

"And that was okay with her?"

Ethan shrugged. "She hasn't contacted him since." Reading the look on her face, he added, "Not even after Matthew's death. She wouldn't be any use to this case. I doubt she even knew her son had health issues."

Sophie exhaled. "Sounds like an open and shut case to me. Is there a reason you had to reassure yourself that I stayed focused?"

"Because I don't think it's that open and shut."

"Meaning?"

"Vanessa Johnson looks like a loving suburban housewife. She's smart, polite, and beautiful."

"You're saying because she's kind and gentle, she'll appeal to women and her loveliness will appeal to men, meaning that a jury could be swayed." Sophie paused, picked up her wine glass and shrugged. "That might be an issue, but frankly, with the amount of evidence mounted against her, I think the jury will be more swayed by a murdered young boy."

"Still, I'm asking you for your best effort at this. I know in my gut she's guilty, and I want her put away."

"So do I."

They sat there in taut silence for a while, before she spoke again. "I bet Dr. Johnson is wishing he hadn't ordered that autopsy so quickly. Although, I do understand how a loved one, especially a father would want to bury his son as quickly as possible."

"He didn't rush that autopsy for the sake of funeral arrangements," Ethan said. "I think he knew his son was being poisoned. He just needed the proof."

She was thoughtful for a moment, and then finally, she nodded and said softly, "I'll start preparing."

"Thank you."

She turned to Jason and noticed as he passed a look between her and Ethan. When his arresting gaze landed on her, she lowered her head.

"And on that note," Jason said, rising. "I think I'll take a break to the restroom. Order me the steak medium, honey."

She nodded, watched him as he headed to the restroom, and feigned interest in the menu.

"Greenville High."

She looked up and saw Ethan trailing the rim of the bourbon glass with his finger, his eyes fixed on the golden-brown liquid. Then they slowly lifted to her, and she saw the well of memories in his eyes.

"We went to high school together. You have a twin sister named Angela."

"That's right," she said.

"Sophie," he said, leaning forward. "It's me. Ethan."

"Yes. You said that. Listen, I'm sorry. It was such a long time ago, and I really don't want to talk about high school."

"Well, actually, I wasn't going to talk about high school. I was thinking about that Fourth of July back in—"

"No."

"No?"

She said it again, this time as a plea and a whisper. "No."

Disappointment clouded his eyes, but he nodded, leaned back to study the menu and she did her best to shut away the memories. Yes, this was most definitely Ethan. But for the sake of her marriage and her sanity, she would go on pretending as though she barely remembered him, when in actuality, he and that summer with him had never been far from her mind.

CHAPTER FIVE

When Sergeant Hailey Cross saw the body lying in the tub, she muttered an expletive and something about the world going to hell. But that was for the benefit of the uniforms and medical personnel milling about. What she really wanted to say was: "Congratulations, Angela. It looks like you finally pissed off the wrong person."

But she didn't say anything out of respect for Ethan standing only a few feet away and her sister, Sophia, waiting in the hall.

She watched Ethan out of the corner of her eye as the medical examiner went over the details of the body. He looked so tired and weary as he leaned against the doorjamb just outside the bathroom with his hands tucked in the pocket of his jeans, but she supposed that was normal considering he was staring down at the body of a woman he had known since he was a teenager.

When the medical examiner finished his preliminary report, Hailey noted the estimated time of death as well as cause of death, gave the medical personnel the official okay to remove the body, and then turned to Ethan.

Ethan returned her gaze and then frowned. "I think this is the first time I've ever seen you wearing makeup. I hope I didn't interrupt a date or something."

She ignored that remark. "Do you have any idea what happened here?"

"No."

She waved a hand toward the ransacked bedroom and sitting area. "Someone was looking for something. We have people at her place, and they're reporting it's also been torn apart. Any idea what this person might have been looking for?"

"All I did was answer the phone, Hailey."

"Why did she call you?"

Ethan looked about to answer but paused at the sight of Angela's body being lifted from the tub and placed in the black body bag set for the morgue, and at that moment, Hailey wished more than anything she could read thoughts.

"Ethan?"

"What?"

"I asked about your phone call from Sophia Arnold."

He nodded, seemingly trying to get his emotions under control. "She called me at home. She said Angela was dead. I got her location and came right over."

"Why did she call you and not 9-1-1?"

"You'll have to ask her."

"Why don't you give us your own guess, Markham."

This came from Hailey's partner, Noah. Sergeant Noah Sayres, with his short buzz haircut and tall lean build always puzzled Hailey. He had a touch of the optimism one would expect from a cop with less than three years on the force, but behind those brown eyes, she detected the sadness of a man who had seen much more than he was willing to admit. She saw that look in a lot of cops, especially those working homicide. She even saw it in herself sometimes when she came home to an empty apartment, drank half a bottle of wine, and had the courage to look at herself in the mirror.

Ethan, who never seemed to warm to the young cop, responded coolly. "I'm not about to guess anything, Sayres. Ask her yourself."

"Fine. Save it for your interview." Noah stepped forward. "The fact that you're standing here observing our investigation is already crossing the line."

"How's that? I'm a cop responding to a situation."

"You're not on duty, and this isn't just any situation. You knew the victim."

They glared at one another as he left the rest unsaid, but Hailey knew what he was getting at. It was rumored that Angela was featuring Ethan in a story that would supposedly shed light on his partner's murder. Now Angela is dead, and that story is nowhere to be found. So far, he had the biggest motive.

Hailey stepped between them and motioned for Ethan to follow her. "Can I speak to you for a minute?"

She led him out of the hotel room. In the corridor, they regarded one another, all too aware that Sophie was several feet away. She was sitting down now, her knees bunched up to her chest, clutching her cell phone in both hands. When she saw the two of them, she looked as though she'd been sucker-punched to the gut. Her face was one of patent despair at losing the other half of herself.

Hailey spared her a momentary glance and then spoke to Ethan in a hushed whisper. "Listen, he might be a jerk, but he's right. You shouldn't be here. I want you to come down to the department to give your official statement, then go home. You've already been implicated in one murder, and that's one too many."

He shook his head. "I'm seeing this through. If nothing

else, I owe her dad justice for his daughter. Besides, I've got nothing to hide."

She angled her head slightly in Sophie's direction. "You think she does?"

She watched him toss the thought around and for a split second, she saw that he was remembering something—something he wasn't yet ready to tell her.

He shook his head. "I can't begin to guess her motives. Never could."

Hailey sighed. "I believe what you said in your statement, Ethan, but that's not why I'm recommending a lawyer to you. This isn't over by any means. It'll be in your best interest to have counsel in the coming days and weeks."

He nodded. "I got it."

Having got that bit of advice off her chest, she called to an officer, who was helping with canvassing the hotel guests. The process was nearly over since this wasn't exactly the busy tourist season.

"I need you to take Mrs. Arnold down to the station and keep her comfortable until her attorney gets there. I'll meet you there."

"No problem, Hailey," he said and walked over to where Sophie was sitting and spoke to her quietly.

They watched as he helped her to her feet and led her past them and down the corridor. Hailey didn't miss the look that passed between her and Ethan and pounced on it as soon as Sophie and the officer were out of earshot.

"What was that about?"

"I want to observe the interview with her," Ethan said, ignoring her question.

She started to protest, but he held up a hand and continued. "Just to observe. She'll have her lawyer there with her, and they don't have to know I'm there. There's something screwed up about this whole thing, and I want to hear what she knows about it."

Hailey continued to stare at Ethan, and the cynical cop in her began wondering if he was interested in what Sophie had to stay, or more specifically, what she had to say that could incriminate him.

"Did you touch anything?"

His face grew hard. "Don't insult me, Hailey."

She waved a hand toward the door. "Wait with one of the uniforms out here until I'm done in there."

Ethan shook his arm free when one of the officers tried to escort him away. "I want in on this. I was first on scene—"

"But not as a cop. Right now, you're just a witness that needs to be questioned."

"You mean a suspect."

"Oh, give me a break, Ethan! You know the routine. You'll get your chance to tell your side of it, but until then, I need to conduct an investigation, so just wait out here!"

He stalked away with one of the officers trailing him and nearly plowed into Sergeant Sayres. Ethan mumbled something unintelligible, but from the scowl that crossed Sayres's face, it wasn't "Excuse me."

Noah watched him walk away and then turned toward Hailey. "What's he got to say?"

"He responded to a phone call from Sophia Arnold to come here."

"She called him?" Noah asked with a frown.

"Exactly what I thought."

"You think he's lying?"

She shrugged. "Not outright lying. Just not giving the whole story, and that really pisses me off, because now I have to wonder what he's trying to hide."

Noah said nothing to that as they entered the hotel room

again and went into the bathroom. The two of them donned latex gloves and knelt beside the tub.

"No blood. Did the M.E. rule it as a drowning?" Noah asked.

"And strangulation. Most likely he had his hands around her throat and pushed her under."

"Witnesses?" Noah asked.

"I've got officers canvassing the hotel staff and other guests downstairs in the lobby. The entire hotel was sealed off, but you know what good that'll do."

Hailey watched as he rose to his feet and tore off the gloves with hands that shook a little.

"The door doesn't look forced open," Noah said.

Hailey thought about it. "It's hard to break into hotel rooms these days. Either she let him in or he had a key. The hotel staff has agreed to let us see the video feed from tonight. They should be cueing that up now."

"Hailey."

Both she and Noah turned at the sound of her name as one of the uniformed officers entered the bathroom with a frown.

"We've got a problem. All footage from five this afternoon until about an hour ago has been removed."

"Come again?" Noah asked, stepping forward.

The officer looked between the two of them, shaking his head. "We don't have video before or after the time of death."

Hailey stepped forward, feeling her jaw tighten and blood pressure rise. "How is that possible?"

"I don't know but we might have a lead. Two of the employees at the front desk say another employee, Josh Carelli, left work early. He said he didn't feel well but seemed nervous and on edge all day. They say he kept hanging around the front desk, flirting with one of the new girls, then all of a sudden he had to go home."

Hailey removed her latex gloves and pinched the bridge of her nose. "All right, get me everyone's names, addresses and phone numbers, including this Josh Carelli. I'll contact them myself."

"I've already got them for you." The officer handed her a sheet of paper with a list of names and addresses and then turned and left.

Noah gestured to the sheet of paper. "You think it's anything?"

She shrugged. "It can't hurt. We need to get back and question Angela's sister. I'm sure she's already lawyered up by now."

"She's a lawyer herself, and she's witnessed quite a few of our interrogation techniques."

"You forgot to add she was married to the master interrogator himself," Hailey said.

Noah sighed. "I didn't want to scare you shitless, so I left that part out. What do you want to do about Ethan?"

Hailey took one last look around the bathroom. She then stepped out into the mess of the living area and watched as the crime scene personnel photographed and logged all evidence.

"He wanted to watch the interrogation with Sophie. I agreed." She held up a hand to stifle any protests from Noah. "Ethan knows all of our techniques too, so the best way to handle him is to not spook him into thinking he's a suspect. Let's just watch and see what he does."

CHAPTER SIX

Three months earlier…
"Remember when Mom would take us on day trips to Sausalito? The ferry ride was the best part."

Sophie nodded, and at the mention of their mother, felt the sudden ache and desperate need to have her by her side right now. There was so much going on, so much that was overwhelming, and it would have been just the comfort she needed to hear her mother say: "Everything's going to work out just fine, Sophie."

"Let's go get a table," Angela said. "I want to show you something."

She followed her inside the ferry to a sitting area with several booths. There, they chose one table by the window and sat across from each other.

"Here," Angela said, sliding a manila folder toward her.

Sophie eyed her and opened the folder, which had several press clippings inside, and then read one sensational headline after another.

Mistrial Declared in Johnson Case.

SFPD Sergeant Involved in Affair with Defendant.

Johnson Case Ends with Murder/Suicide.

SFPD Sergeant Found Murdered.

SFPD Sergeant Implicated in Partner's Murder.

She slowly closed the folder and looked out at the bay as the ferry made its journey from San Francisco to Sausalito and tried not to succumb to all the pain that trial brought to her life, her career, and her marriage.

"I've been following you, twin," Angela said.

Sophie mustered a laugh. "Is that why you came here? For a story? Our town news made it all the way to Los Angeles?"

"I came because I knew you needed me. And yes, partly for the story. It was a big case, Sophie. Journalists every-where are drooling over it. A murdered young boy with his stepmother as the prime suspect was sensational enough. Now, it's revealed her arresting officer was involved with her? People can't get enough of it."

"Well the story is pretty much dead now, isn't it?"

She instantly regretted her choice of words, considering what had happened to Jason, Vanessa, and Carl, not to mention little Matthew. Death seemed to surround that case from the beginning. If Sophie had been the superstitious type, she would have been convinced the whole event was cursed.

Angela gave her a pointed look. "It's now all the more thrilling."

"You're here to write a story about my husband and his lover. You do know I was a suspect in their murder investigation? Christ, Angie, the SFPD couldn't wait to bust my door down and take me in for the murder of one of their own. Whether he cheated on me or not didn't matter. He died a cop, and as far as they were concerned, I was the scorned wife who killed him and his lover."

"And they finally realized you couldn't have done it." She seemed to hesitate for a moment before continuing. "I wasn't sure if I should tell you this or not, but I have a source who claims they have evidence of Jason's killer. But there's a catch."

Sophie stared, silently willing for her to spit it out.

"They say it's Ethan."

Without responding, she turned her head toward the window, not wanting Angela to see evidence on her face of the conflict that was warring inside her. She had been afraid this day would come.

"Who's your source?"

"You know I can't tell you that. I can tell you they're very credible, and the evidence they have is undeniable. The source says Ethan was the last to see him alive. And apparently, they fought, because the Coroner's report shows Jason had defensive wounds."

"So why haven't they gone to the police with it?"

"Without revealing too much, let's just say my source is worried the information may get back to Ethan. Do you think he could have done it?"

Sophie avoided her eyes again. "He was there."

"That wasn't my question, Sophie. I know about all the evidence against him, but this is Ethan. Ethan with the hypnotizing gray eyes. Ethan, your first real love. Do you believe he killed Jason?"

She finally did look at her sister and for a moment, just stared into the face of a woman who was the mirror image of herself. For weeks now, she'd been trying to rid the thought from her mind that Ethan would ever be involved in Jason's murder. But there were so many questions he had yet to answer.

Finally, she shook her head. "I don't know."

"Well maybe, he'll enlighten me on what actually happened that last night he was with Jason. I offered to meet him for drinks this week, but unfortunately, I had to postpone because I need to fly back to L.A. to follow up a lead."

Sophie's eyes widened. "You made a date with him?"

"It's not a date, it's drinks. As soon as I got into town, I looked him up, and he agreed to meet with me. He deserves to tell his side of the story. With all the evidence I have, I still don't have motive."

"Well, maybe you'll find one. He always did open up to you more than me." Sophie paused for a moment and then continued with resolve. "I want to help you. Whether Ethan is the killer or not, I want to help find Jason's murderer. Tell me what I can do."

Angela sighed and grabbed the back of her neck. "Listen, I know you're trying to be the good wife and give your deceased husband some justice, but frankly, Jason doesn't deserve it. He cheated on you, humiliated you and nearly cost you your career. Besides, if it really came down to it, could you really prosecute Ethan?"

"Just because he used to work for dad doesn't make him innocent."

"But he didn't just work for Dad. The two of you were…" Angela paused and frowned. "What am I missing? Did something happen between the two of you?"

Sophie ignored that. "You already have a source telling you Ethan did it. You won't tell me who this person is, but they gave you concrete evidence."

"It's all circumstantial. I'm not going to publish a story that accuses a man of murder based on that."

She sat back and narrowed her eyes. "Maybe I should be the one asking if something happened between the two of you."

Angela also chose to ignore that remark. "I'll call you when I need your help. We have a few weeks at least. I'll reschedule my meeting with Ethan when I get back from

L.A." She rose from the table. "I'm going to use the restroom before we dock. I also need a cup of coffee. You want anything?"

She shook her head and once again gave the blue water her attention. Moments passed before she felt a soft hand on her shoulder, causing her to turn and look up into her sister's eyes.

"This is murder, Sophie. Please be sure of your decision before you go down this road. Jason definitely doesn't deserve your loyalty."

"No, he doesn't, but I'm giving it to him anyway."

Her eyes turned sad as she walked away toward the ladies' room. Sophie couldn't tell her the true reason she was so hell-bent on bringing Jason's killer to justice. She wasn't being a loyal wife. She was being a guilty wife. She looked down at the folder of articles Angela left and then pushed them away from her. The force of it caused Angela's cell to also push across the small table and fall to the floor. She bent down to pick it up, not even realizing Angela had left it behind. She placed it back on the table and looked out at the scenery drifting by. Then she looked down at the phone again, trying to keep up with her racing thoughts.

* * *

Sophie came away from the memory, looked to Sergeant Hailey Cross, and decided she didn't like the way the woman regarded her with those cool blue eyes. She had the feeling she'd already been deemed guilty. Sergeant Noah Sayres, on the other hand, didn't seem to be sure at all about her innocence or guilt, but he still held the cold gaze very well.

"Mrs. Arnold—" Cross began.

"It's James now," Sophie interrupted. "I went back to my maiden name."

Hailey made a quick note in a folder, before continuing. "Ms. James, let me start by saying how sorry I am for your loss."

Sophie acknowledged the condolences with a brief nod and braced herself for a quick blow that was sure to follow.

"According to your statement, you were at Franklin Hotel because Angela asked to meet you there."

"That's correct. Angela called my cell earlier today while I was at work and asked that I meet her at Franklin Hotel at seven."

"Can you tell me about your day before you arrived at Franklin Hotel?"

"I returned calls and emails, conducted a deposition, and had a meeting with a judge and defense attorney about an upcoming case."

"So, besides the call from Angela asking you to meet that evening, nothing out of the ordinary happened?"

"What can I do for you, Sergeant?"

"Tell me what she's up to."

"Who?"

"I don't have a lot of time to waste, Sophie. Don't play games with me. You know who I'm talking about."

"I have a full day of depositions, and a brief that needs to be rewritten by the end of the day. If you're not going to get to the point—"

"Angela is supposedly doing a story about Jason's death. Rumor has it she's got a source naming me as the killer."

"I heard that rumor too."

"Only you know if it's true or not."

Sophie didn't say a word, but turned to stand by her door, signaling for him to leave. "Please don't make me call security."

He stared at her in disbelief and then shook his head and laughed. "I don't know why I expected more from you." He headed toward the door and then stopped next to her, his large frame, which seemed to take up what was left of the small space in the room, now towered over her. "She's in way over her head. You tell her I said that."

"Ms. James," Hailey said, prodding her.

"No," Sophie said, keeping her face expressionless. "It was a pretty uneventful day."

"Did Angela say why she wanted to meet you?"

"No."

"You stated you arrived at the hotel a little after eight thirty." Hailey paused from reading her notes to look up at Sophie. "Why were you so late?"

"My workload keeps me busy. I told Angela as much and said I probably wouldn't be able to make it by seven, but would get there as soon as I could."

"And she didn't mention or even hint at what the secret hotel meeting was all about?"

"She's already answered that Sergeant Cross," Brandon, her lawyer interjected.

He was an old law school friend from Berkeley she had called to sit in on this interview with her.

Hailey continued, seemingly undaunted by the interruption. "Walk me through what happened when you got to the hotel."

She breathed in and out and then began reciting what she'd rehearsed while sitting in that hotel corridor.

"Angie left me a key card at the desk with her room number, so I went to the desk first, showed the clerk my identification, received the key card, and went straight to the elevators."

Sophie's heels were muffled as she walked along the carpeted floor toward Angela's room. She was going to make this quick, and this time she'd be sure her sister understood once and for all that she wasn't her puppet. What was she doing in this hotel anyway? Why couldn't they just meet at a restaurant or even Sophie's place?

Room 722. Sophie inserted the key card she'd been given by the desk clerk into the lock. The green light flashed, and she turned the handle.

"Stop."

Sophie looked up at Hailey's raised hand.

"She left you a key card at the front desk?"

"That's right."

"Why didn't she just have you knock?"

Sophie shrugged. "Maybe she figured it was more convenient that way."

"Is that what the two of you normally did?"

"No Sergeant. We never met in a hotel room before for any reason."

"So why now?"

Sophie let out a breath. "All I know is that this was important, and she didn't want us meeting publicly."

Hailey's gaze never wavered. "Go on."

Sophie glanced around the room and noticed Angela's favorite handbag was tossed aside and all the contents dumped on the floor. She looked to the bedroom and saw the mattress on the bed had been overturned, dresser drawers and nightstand drawers were opened, hotel stationery was strewn all over the desk. What the hell happened here? She looked up and saw the closed door ahead, leading to what must be the bathroom.

She knocked on the bathroom door. "Angie, I'm here. Are you all right? This place is a mess."

No answer came from the other side.

Sophie knocked again. "It's been a long day, Angie. Come out so we can talk. I want to get home and go to bed."

But there was still no answer. Irritated, Sophie turned the knob and pushed her way into the bathroom.

"It was dark, but I could still see her from the light that illuminated the living area," she said. "I was angry because I thought she was ignoring me, so I felt for a light switch along the wall and turned it on."

She stopped, took a deep breath, and tried to steady her voice. "Angie was in the tub and…" She stared past them, still seeing the lifeless form in the tub. "Her face, her lips were so blue."

"That's enough, Sergeant," her lawyer said. "You know the rest."

"Actually, no I don't," Hailey countered. "That part needs clarification, too. You saw it was your sister. Then what?"

"I—I don't think I did anything for a moment. I just stood there, not believing it was her. Then all of a sudden, I got scared, thinking whoever did that to her could still be somewhere in the room. I ran from the bathroom. I remember stumbling on something and fell to the floor on my hands and knees. I got up and ran out of the room. I got as far as the elevators and realized I couldn't just leave her like that. I needed to get help. So, I called…"

She trailed off, knowing what was coming next; knowing that Hailey Cross had been salivating to get to this part of the interrogation.

"You called Sergeant Markham."

Silence followed for several seconds and when she realized Sophie wasn't going to say anything to that, she continued.

"Did you call your sister ahead of time to let her know you were on your way?" she asked.

She recognized the question for the trap it was. Having observed countless interviews and beyond familiar with police procedure, she knew they would waste no time in obtaining Angela's cell phone records, even go through the phone itself.

"Yes. I called her about thirty minutes before I arrived,

letting her know I was on my way, but she didn't answer. I'm sure you have a record of my calling her."

Hailey plowed on. "What was this secret meeting about anyway?"

"Sergeant," Brandon warned.

"You two ladies have apartments of your own. What was she afraid of?"

"She wasn't afraid of anything," I replied.

Hailey leaned forward in her chair, resting her forearms on the table that separated them.

"Let's get back to your call to Sergeant Markham. You let yourself inside the hotel room, called out to your sister, with no answer. Then you find her in the bathtub."

"That's right."

"You run back out to the hall, throw up your lunch, pull out your cell phone and dial, not 9-1-1, but Sergeant Markham." Hailey paused and frowned. "I'm confused. You find your sister dead, and you don't call 9-1-1?"

"He was the first person that came to my mind. Angie and I have known Ethan, I mean Sergeant Markham since we were kids."

"Tell me why the room was ransacked."

"I have no idea."

"I think you do. I think you two shared a lot that you don't want to tell me, including the topic of your little meeting this evening, but I'm going to venture a guess and say it had something to do with the story she was working on involving Sergeant Markham and this police department."

"All right, let's go." Brandon stood, grabbed his briefcase and her coat from behind her chair. Sophie stood more slowly but still stared at Hailey as she continued talking.

"There are a lot of rumors floating around about that story and how explosive it would be—more than likely put some cops and higher officials in jail. Are you telling me that an ambitious ADA like yourself wouldn't be in the thick of that? Everyone in the city knows what a career climber you are, Ms. James. But that last big trial you did, the Vanessa Johnson case, right? That mistrial screwed everything up for you. This was your chance to get it right this time, wasn't it?"

"I said let's go," Brandon demanded.

Sophie wrenched her arm free from his grasp and put her hands on the table and leaned toward Hailey, her eyes glaring.

"I called Sergeant Markham, because he was the first person that came to my mind. Whether it's strange or not, it's the truth. You can think what you want about me, but if my sister was killed because she planned to out a few cops, then I suggest you quit trying to get dirt from me and start questioning your colleagues."

She turned to follow Brandon out of the room.

"I know what you did."

Sophie stopped halfway out of the room and turned to look back at Sergeant Cross.

"Excuse me?"

She pulled a sheet of paper from the manila folder. "We requested a copy of Angela's phone records, but in the meantime, out tech guys were able to unlock her phone and it appears that the last text message she sent was to you." Hailey read from the sheet of paper. "I know what you did. Why Sophie?"

Hailey paused to look at her with an arched brow. "Do you want to tell us what it is you did, Ms. James?"

Instead of answering, she finally allowed Brandon to lead her out of the interrogation room, and they waded their way through the sea of cubicles toward the elevators. When the elevator arrived, they stepped inside, and Sophie leaned against Brandon out of tiredness and frustration. He put a comforting arm around her shoulders, and she looked up at him with a grateful smile. Then she noticed Ethan watching them through the open doors, and the smile she wore fell away and was replaced with a mixture of shock, anger, and embarrassment. Had he been listening to her interview the entire time? She opened her mouth to say something, but not exactly sure what. Then the elevator doors closed before she could utter a single word, and she was staring at her own blurred reflection.

CHAPTER SEVEN

*B*randon suggested Sophie leave her car at the hotel until morning and then offered to drive her home. But she refused, needing the quiet time to herself, and let him take her back to the Franklin Hotel for her car. She called her father and stepmother while at the precinct. Hearing Cynthia's sobs and the catch in her father's voice was too much for her to bear. Needless to say, she didn't tell them that she had been brought in for questioning, that she was the one who'd found Angela, that they'd agreed to meet or that the reason she may have been killed was because she was trying to find Jason's killer.

She pulled up to the steep driveway of the house she once shared with him, turned the car off, and sat there for a long time in silence. She then reached in her purse, pulled out her cell phone, and scrolled to the last text message she'd received from Angela, which Sergeant Cross had mentioned.

I know what you did. Why Sophie?

The tears she had been holding back from the moment she found her in that hotel bathtub couldn't be contained any longer. It was a slow trickle at first, and then they were streaming uncontrollably, staining her cheeks, and finally a sob tore from her throat. She pounded the steering wheel with her fists over and over again, letting the anger and grief consume her. Then she let go a scream that was loud and long. She screamed at the top of her lungs, until her throat felt scratchy and hoarse, and didn't care if the neighbors could hear her through the closed car windows.

"Goddammit, Angie!"

She screamed again and then heaved in and out, trying to catch her breath, and it suddenly occurred to her that she never showed this much emotion when Jason was killed. Then again, she and her husband had never been as close as she and Angela had been, and she didn't know whether that made her proud or sad.

She took several more deep breaths, gathered the strength to pull herself from the car, and went inside where memories of Jason awaited her. There was still so much of him that she never bothered to toss: photos, DVDs, a worn favorite Giants shirt, his SFPD badge. She didn't know whether she was keeping them out of love or because she just didn't have the energy to box everything up. She thought about how she would have to move everything out of the apartment that Angela had rented, as well as make time to fly to L.A. and box up the rest of her things. The thought of the tasks that lay ahead of her nearly broke her again.

Once inside the house, Sophie threw her coat and messenger bag onto Jason's armchair and practically fell onto the sofa. She leaned her head back and thought of everything she didn't tell Sergeant Cross.

She'd lied about the reason she had called Ethan. The truth was, she called him because she wanted to see if he would answer. A small part of her that refused to be silenced wondered if he could have done this. She didn't tell his colleagues about his visit to her that afternoon and how angry he had been. Nor, did she tell them that the two of them had a more intimate history than that of childhood friends and that as the weeks past, leading up to the trial, Sophie had become more and more nervous to be around him.

"So, we're clear? All you need to do is stick to the facts. When I or defense counsel ask you a question, just answer honestly and succinctly."

Ethan was nodding his head before Sophie even finished her orders.

"I know the drill when it comes to court proceedings, Sophie. This isn't my first trial."

She looked away and made a fuss about clearing her desk of paperwork, not sure why she suddenly felt embarrassed around him.

He was sitting in her visitor's chair as they made believe it was the witness stand he would be sitting in by tomorrow morning. This afternoon, she'd called his desk phone and asked that he drop by her office that evening so she could coach him on what to say. He sounded annoyed, but she knew he just wanted this trial over and done with, for Vanessa Johnson to be convicted of murdering her stepson, and for Carl Johnson to finally see it all come to an end so he could mourn his son in peace. Ethan accepted her invitation and was in her office at six thirty on the dot to begin his mock testimony. But after an hour of sharing a close space with him, old memories were beginning to resurface, and she was regretting her decision.

She kept busy with shuffling papers on her desk. "You misunderstood me, Ethan. I wasn't trying to imply you couldn't do your job."

"Then stop with the condescension."

Sophie whirled around. "I wasn't being condescending. I just want you to be prepared for the questions that are going to be thrown at you. The jury takes a cop's account of things very seri-

ously. They see you as someone who can be trusted, and the defense attorney is going to do his best to dismantle your credibility. He'll even try to rile you by questioning your investigative techniques."

"Do you?" he asked.

"Do I what?"

He rose from his seat, but continued to look at her. "Trust me."

"What are you talking about?"

"Do you trust me?"

"Yes."

"Then believe me when I tell you this isn't my first trial. I want a guilty verdict just as much as you do. Maybe for different reasons, but we both want it. I won't screw it up."

"Different reasons?"

He looked around at the boxes still piled in one corner of her office.

"Still moving?"

"Yes, after I close out this trial."

He nodded. "It seems you have a lot to lose if this doesn't go your way."

Sophie knew what he was insinuating. He believed she was only working this trial for a career boost, but she decided to let it go.

"Like you said: I'll have to trust you and Jason to do your parts."

His eyes flickered at the mention of Jason, but he didn't say anything, and she couldn't guess what he was thinking. Suddenly, she realized they were standing very close to one another. He must have realized it too, because they both backed away from each other at the same time.

She cleared her throat as a way of clearing the tension that managed to come out of nowhere. "I've taken up enough of your time. Go. I'm sure you have plans for your Friday evening anyway."

He shook his head slowly. "No, actually I haven't made any plans. I was just going to catch a movie and grab something to eat afterwards."

She gave a wry smile. "Exciting."

"You interested?"

Her smile instantly fell away as though he'd flipped an internal switch. She gaped at him, and for several moments, the ensuing silence was all that floated between them.

Then he had the grace to look horrified. "Sorry. I didn't mean that how it sounded. I meant I have a friend I can ask to join us and you can call Jason. We can make it a double date."

"No, it's not that. I just—I've got to go through the defense witness list again and make sure I've got all my questions lined up."

"It's okay, Sophie."

She started to fumble with papers again and could now add awkward to the embarrassment she was feeling.

As she started to walk away, Ethan gently grabbed her arm and turned her to face him. "Fourth of July, 2002. I know you remember."

For a moment, she stayed silent, hoping he could see in her eyes the plea for him to drop the subject entirely. But he only returned her stare with the silent response that he wasn't going to back down.

With a sigh, she admitted, "I do." Then a pause. "Are you going to tell Jason?"

"What would be the point?"

"So why bring it up?"

"Because whether you believe me or not, that day, that summer, meant something to me, and I'll be damned if you're going to walk around me, pretending it didn't mean something to you, too."

She released her arm from his grasp. "I think it's time for you to go, Sergeant. Don't keep your date waiting."

CHAPTER EIGHT

It was nearly one thirty in the morning before Hailey finally admitted to herself that she was dozing more than working at her desk. She'd worked well past her shift that evening and would have stayed much longer if she wasn't so conscious about making sure her colleagues knew she had a life.

So about two hours after her shift ended, she drove home, all the while eager to review the evidence her team had uncovered from the hotel room once she got to her own home office.

Sophie James had no idea why her sister was meeting her in a hotel room, the desk clerk Josh Carelli was nowhere to be found, the digital camera footage was MIA, and the night hotel manager, Anita Sykes, was apparently out of town and not checking her voicemails—or just ignoring them. This case was already giving her a headache with all its loose ends.

But truth be told, Hailey wasn't interested in finding Angela's killer. Like every cop in the homicide division who believed the rumor mill, she wanted her hands on that story. For weeks leading up to her death, it was circulating that

Angela, a reporter for the *San Francisco Chronicle* was writing a tell-all story about the SFPD—specifically the homicide division and how it covered up the murder of one of its own. There were also rumblings that she had a source, and that source knew the identity of Jason's killer. The Captain of the homicide division, the Deputy Chief of the SFPD, and even the Internal Affairs Division threatened the *Chronicle* with every legal action imaginable if they didn't force Angela to reveal her source and have him or her brought in for questioning. The phrases "impeding an investigation" and "obstruction of justice" were thrown around so much, even Hailey got sick of hearing it. But the *Chronicle* had top brass and lawyers of its own and refused to admit to anything that was, after all, only a rumor.

As the weeks passed, the whispers grew louder, the threats more serious, but no explosive article was ever released. Now tonight, the reporter who was supposedly writing the story had turned up dead. By morning, the news of Angela's death will have swept across the city and even into L.A. since she was still based there, and the press was going to demand answers. Hailey didn't envy the public relations department at this moment, but her job wasn't any easier. She and Noah were tasked with finding the murderer. Between the press and a very emotional and blunt phone call from Larry James, Angela's father, it was made clear that the cold case files would not be an option.

She had a job to do, and the reason she was a damned good cop, the reason she'd risen so quickly through the ranks was because she'd learned to shut those feelings out and put her job first. So, she gritted her teeth and before her interview with Sophie James, she and Noah conducted a search of Angela's apartment. Yet it turned out there was nothing overtly suspicious about anything they found.

The only promising item her team had come across was a

laptop, and at first glance, they only found past and current stories she'd been working on. It would take weeks to go through every file on the hard drive, but Hailey didn't have weeks. They'd even rushed the autopsy to tomorrow so the body could be released to the family for burial. Angela had acquired more power in her short time here in San Francisco than Hailey had been able to pull in her more than fifteen years as a cop.

But what about Ethan? What was his role in all of this? It was confirmed he knew Angela and Sophie James as teenagers, grew up and became partners with Sophie's husband, then, in a curious twist of fate, became the number one suspect in his partner's murder. Too much history. She was absolutely certain Ethan knew about the story Angela was planning to write, but was the story supposed to exonerate him as Jason's alleged killer or outright accuse him? If the latter, that would be a strong motive for Ethan to get rid of his long-time friend.

She admitted she had never been able to read Ethan. Since his transfer from the Missing Persons department to Homicide, he'd hit the ground running with his first big case, Matthew Johnson's murder. She and a lot of cops in the division had been surprised the Lieutenant assigned such a high-profile case to Jason and his new partner, but Ethan's reputation of closing cases and getting convictions in Missing Persons had preceded him. The Lieutenant was looking for a big win, and he was certain Sergeant Ethan Markham would bring him one. Yes, Hailey was impressed with his work ethic, but she hated that he seemed to play everything close to his chest. She was certain he would reveal details only when he was ready for her to have them.

But the one person she knew she had pegged was Angela's twin sister, Sophia, Sophie as she preferred to be called, which Hailey found ironic because no one could ever get close enough, much less friendly enough with the woman to use her preferred nickname. To every cop in the division, she had been Mrs. Arnold.

On one hand, Hailey respected her, because together they shared the bond of two women trying to prove themselves in professions dominated by men. And after that whole debacle with Jason and Vanessa, she grudgingly admitted that Sophie handled herself with dignity. But on the other hand, she wouldn't put anything past the ambitious ADA. She was certain that under the right circumstances, that woman could be very cunning.

She thought back to the interview and how calm and collected Sophie had been. "Yes," "No," "I don't recall." It was like pulling teeth and when Hailey did finally get her to elaborate, it was like a game of semantics. She'd never been so mentally exhausted after an interview. But it felt damn good to get the last word in and rile Sophie before she left.

That text message.

Hailey flipped to the sheet of paper in a folder and read over the message once again. She noticed all previous texts from Angela had been urgent pleas to get Sophie to the hotel. Then Sophie replied she'd be late.

Hailey frowned to herself as she realized that instead of responding to Sophie's text about being late, she simply typed: *I know what you did.*

Something had happened in those few hours to make Angela say that. What did Angela find out about her sister and was the answer somewhere in that hotel room?

CHAPTER NINE

When Ethan walked into Tanya Wallace's cramped office the next morning, she looked up, tore off her glasses, and gave him a baleful look.

He raised his hands in mock surrender. "Is that how you receive all your guests?"

"Don't say anything to me. Just turn around and walk back out the door."

He grinned. "Hailey talked to you, didn't she?"

"Hailey Cross, Lieutenant Walker, and everybody else and their grandfather has come through this office, telling me I shouldn't be telling or showing you anything except the nearest exit."

"Since when did you start taking orders?"

She sighed, rose from her desk, and all five feet two inches of her moved in close. She pressed a finger to his chest. "Whether or not the entire homicide department told me not to talk to you, I still have a brain and it's telling me you don't need to be here."

"Angela was a good friend to me."

She took a deep breath and continued in a more even

tone. "Listen, you know I like you, but you're not on this case, and you weren't her family."

"She called me before it happened."

Tanya's eyes softened, and her skin seemed to pale slightly at his words. She then gave him a knowing nod rife with sympathy.

"And you didn't answer," she supplied.

"I was still so angry with her. I don't know why she was calling me, and probably won't ever know. But when I did finally answer, it was her sister on the other line, telling me someone had killed her."

When she didn't say anything more, Ethan continued. "Call it guilt, a sense of duty, whatever. I just want to be able to help. I only want the basic facts. You don't have to tell me anything you don't feel comfortable telling."

She continued to stare at him, but he knew she was weighing the pros and cons inside her head, and to his surprise, she turned around and gestured for him to follow her as she rounded her desk and sat down facing her computer. As she pulled up Angela's file, Ethan looked around the small space that was the office of the Medical Examiner. Tanya had been appointed Deputy M.E. after Carl Johnson's death. He noticed the framed picture on the wall of Johnson in a white lab coat, looking professional and distinguished with a plaque that read: *In Memoriam.*

Okay here we go," Tanya said, bringing his attention back to her. "Time of death is estimated to have been between seven and nine in the evening, cause of death was strangulation and asphyxiation by water."

"Can you tell if she was killed before she went into the water?" he asked, leaning over her shoulder to read the notes.

"She was alive when she went underwater."

"There was a bruise on her left cheek. Can you tell me if—"

"Hold on. I'm getting to it," she said, scrolling down in the document. "Bruising on the right cheek indicates assailant is left handed and swelling of cheek indicates wound was inflicted at about the same time of drowning."

"She fought with the killer." Ethan balled his left fist and mocked a swing. "He hits her in the face, the blow weakens her, and he continues to hold her under the water. Did you find anything under her fingernails?"

Tanya shook her head. "If she fought back, she didn't make contact, or the murderer was thorough enough to clean under her nails. I'm sorry."

Ethan nodded and could tell she was offering condolences for more than just Angela's premature death.

"I appreciate it." He turned to leave but stopped when she called him back.

"I debated whether or not to tell you this, but I think I will. You've been asking the same exact questions she was, and if I told her, I may as well let you know, too."

She rose from the desk and gestured again for him to follow. This time, she led him to refrigeration where Angela's body was kept. She grabbed latex gloves, tossed him a pair, and donned them herself. They entered the cold, sterile room and headed toward the wall of steel drawers. She grabbed one handle and pulled it open with ease. As she lifted the white shroud, Ethan steeled himself and tried not to react at the sight of her lying there, unmoving.

"Ethan?"

He focused his attention on what Tanya pointed to with a gloved hand. There were markings along Angela's neck, most likely bruises from the strangulation. He leaned in for a closer look. After a moment, he looked up and met Tanya's eyes, not certain if what he was seeing was correct.

Do you see it?"

He shook his head in disbelief. "I was there that night, but

I only got a quick glance at her body before I left the room and called it in. I never went back in because I didn't want to disturb the scene. Then when the crime scene unit and your team got there, I wasn't allowed anywhere near the body. But now…"

"From the position her body was in and the hand print on her neck, we've surmised she was strangled from behind. But from the look of this finger pattern, her head was slightly turned when she was attacked.".

"You're saying she may have seen her attacker."

Tanya's silence was confirmation. It still didn't explain if she knew the killer or not. Nevertheless, his mind began spinning with unanswered questions and too many scenarios now that didn't fit.

"I have to go. Thanks again."

He paused at the door and then turned back around. "I guess I don't have to tell you this is between us. I know you said Hailey was already here asking the same questions, but she's a cop and will have my same instincts. Still, my being here will be our secret."

"My lips are sealed," she said, removing the latex gloves. "But I wasn't talking about Sergeant Cross. She was here when I did the autopsy. I'm talking about Sophia James, the victim's twin."

He frowned. "Sophie was here?"

Tanya nodded. "Yeah. She identified the body, of course, and then came back this morning wanting to know every-thing about the autopsy findings, just like you. The only thing that seemed odd to me is that she knew as much about that crime scene as I did." She cocked her head to one side and frowned. "How long do you think she was in that hotel room before you got there?"

* * *

After leaving the M.E.'s office, Ethan returned to his department to get some work done, thinking that keeping busy would help get his mind off Angela's murder, as well as put a dent in the unsolved cases that were cluttering his desk. However, he'd been staring at the computer monitor for nearly an hour, not really seeing the case notes.

He gave his eyes a rest and looked around the cubicle-filled space that made up the homicide division, and to his surprise, he noticed that several pairs of eyes were looking his way. Some immediately looked away in embarrassment, while others openly regarded him with wariness or suspicion. Receiving this kind of attention caused old memories to resurface. It was only months ago he encountered the same looks after Jason was found murdered. More looks followed that turned to outright hostility when it became known he was the last person to see his partner alive. Now, in some weird sense of déjà vu, he was reliving it all again, only the victim was a woman he'd known years ago, and rumor had it, she had a source that named him as Jason's killer, giving him the ultimate motive to kill her.

Ethan wanted to throw something. His luck couldn't be this bad. Two deaths? He was being implicated in two deaths? The Internal Affairs Division was likely chomping at the bit to corner him for an interview. After his first round of questioning shortly after Jason's murder, Ethan retained private counsel just out of caution. That move only heightened the suspicions of the other cops in his division, but he believed in being prepared.

The first thing his lawyer did was advise him to be as honest with him as possible. Following those orders, Ethan told him everything that had happened the night he went to see Jason, including the part about him being alive when he left him.

"Okay, now tell me what you didn't tell IAD," his lawyer said.

Ethan told him the rest of the story, and when his lawyer started hinting at telling Internal Affairs, he shut it down.

"This will get them off your back," he said.

"I didn't do it," Ethan said. "That's all they need to know."

"Yes, and this will prove it."

"Then find another way to prove my innocence."

"Sergeant Markham—"

"Find another way."

The apartment Jason was staying in didn't have working video cameras, and without proper surveillance and only hearsay to go on, the case had gone cold, which was unacceptable when it came to a cop killing—no matter how much embarrassment the cop caused his division. Still, Internal Affairs had to put the case on hold, but then Angela came to San Francisco and the investigative story she was working on had the division looking in his direction once again. Now, she had been murdered, and he was the one with motive to silence her.

He returned his attention to the computer screen and continued on with his work, ignoring the watchful eyes around him. He still had a job to do, despite the suspicion surrounding him. However, it wasn't long before his thoughts turned to Sophie.

He'd tried visiting her countless times following Jason's death, but she refused to see him, and although he knew and understood why, it was still driving him crazy. Jason had been his partner, his friend, despite the shitstorm he caused in his career and personal life. Ethan had grieved for him, too. But he also had carried around the guilt of what happened between him and Sophie that night. He only wanted someone to talk to about it, and she was the only other person in the world who would have understood what he was feeling. But after being stonewalled by her numerous times, Ethan decided to take a hint and give her space to grieve for her husband. But something about Angela's death didn't sit right with him. He may not have killed her, but he knew without a doubt her death was connected in some way to Jason, and the only connection he could think of between Angela and Jason was Sophie. So, this time, he was sorry to say he wouldn't be leaving her alone to grieve. This time, she was going to talk to him.

CHAPTER TEN

The funeral for Angela was held the following Saturday after her body was released from the morgue, and Ethan had to drag himself out of bed. It wasn't from grief—though he felt the pang of sadness at having to say goodbye to a woman he knew from childhood—but from the fact that he didn't want to see so many sad faces. He'd seen those faces before in spades when he had to tell a person someone they loved dearly had been killed. He was now seeing what they went through the days following that news up until the moment they had to finally say goodbye.

He dressed in a simple black suit, white shirt and tie, shaved his three-day-old growth and had his hair trimmed to a length neither too long nor too short. Before he left, he glanced around for his keys and noticed they were on the mantle next to the framed picture of Angela and him. They were having dinner at a little Italian place in North Beach. He opened the camera function on his phone and snagged one of the waiters to take their picture. She'd objected instantly.

"It's been years since we've seen each other," he said. "You were a good friend to me growing up."

"No." Then she smiled shyly. "I really don't like my picture being taken."

"Then I promise to never let you see this," he replied, scooting his chair closer to her and wrapping an arm around her. "All you have to do is smile."

He never meant to get it framed. He'd only planned to keep the photo in his phone as just something to look at every now and then, but when he got home that night and pulled up the image, he found he couldn't stop looking at it. Her smile, her eyes…All he could see was Sophie. All he could see now was Sophie.

He turned away from the photo, but still thinking on that day, he remembered how relieved he'd felt to have someone he could finally talk to. Angela had been his conduit to releasing everything that had been troubling him. Only now, he realized that opening up to her had been his biggest mistake.

* * *

Angela loved white roses and would have laughed with pure joy at the sight of so many. Sophie had the florist decorate her casket with bushels of them. She always said they were simple and classic, not to mention elegant and could make any other flower truly beautiful. Sophie, on the other hand, preferred tulips—bright pink and yellow ones.

"We bow our heads in prayer for the soul of one of God's children," the Pastor Lee intoned. He was the head Pastor of the church her father and Cynthia attended.

While the other attendants obediently bowed their heads, Sophie kept hers raised, still studying the white roses, but not seeing them anymore. Why was she killed? Was it because of that damned story? Did she go too far in her research and find out something she wasn't supposed to discover? Then there was that last text message. She didn't have to guess what she was talking about. She knew what she'd done, and Angela had found out. But how? Maybe Ethan…

The instant thought of him made Sophie turn her head slightly to her right. To her surprise, he was staring right back at her, and she quickly looked away from his arresting gaze. To him, she must look very guilty, but he saw her when she came running out of that room, looking half scared out of her mind. Anyone could surmise she had nothing to do with her sister's death.

She stole another glance among the faces of so many attendants and noticed Hailey Cross was looking at her, too, but also shifting her eyes back and forth between Sophie and Ethan. Sophie could only imagine what she was thinking. She needed to keep her distance from the entire SFPD, specifically its homicide division. That's where Angela's source said the cover up of Jason's murder happened. One of his own colleagues murdered him and the case had deliberately gone cold in order to protect his killer.

She turned back to Ethan, who was still watching her with an unblinking gaze. This time, Sophie didn't flinch or turn away but returned the stare. She had nothing to feel guilty over, nothing to be afraid of. If this mysterious source was to be believed, he was the one who should be looking away in guilt. But like Angela had said on the ferry to Sausalito—this was Ethan.

Pastor Lee ended his prayer and allowed the mourners to step forward to each lay a white rose upon the casket. Sophie and her father stepped forward and they both dropped a rose. Stepping back, Sophie took her father's hand, and she felt him stiffen only so slightly. Then he patted their clasped hands with his free one and slowly pulled his hand free of hers. She didn't know why but with that gesture, she felt compelled to look to Ethan again. His eyes were softer now, and she knew he'd seen the exchange.

The funeral ended, and Sophie and her family began to accept the long line of condolences.

"It was a beautiful service," her father said as he stood beside her. "Thank you for planning it. I just didn't have the energy to think about burying one of my children."

His voice trailed off, and she knew he was struggling to resist the grief and anguish that would soon wash over him.

"It was no trouble, Dad," she said, surreptitiously passing him a tissue, which he accepted with a silent nod.

Cynthia, her father's wife and Sophie's stepmother stepped forward and embraced her. Sophie clung to her, wishing her father would hold her this tight. Then Cynthia pulled away. "You're coming up to the house, right?"

She nodded and Cynthia beamed and then whispered into her ear. "Your father may have trouble showing it, but it means a lot that you're here with him."

Sophie didn't know how to respond to that, so she didn't and simply smiled. While she accepted the myriad of condolences from friends, coworkers, and distant relatives, she turned her head, and without appearing too obvious, looked for Ethan one more time. She sensed he had something on his mind and knew he was trying to get a moment alone with her, but she wasn't going to let that happen. As soon as she could, she was hightailing it out of there. Her father was holding a wake at his home, and only family and close friends were permitted. Even though Ethan was considered a close friend, Sophie made certain no invitation was sent to him. She couldn't risk being cornered by him, forced to look into those cop eyes and answer questions she wasn't yet ready to answer.

She finally spotted him. He must have broken away from the crowd when she wasn't looking, because now he was standing far off by another headstone, and she didn't have to join him to know whose it was.

* * *

Ethan wasn't interested in condolences and walked away from the crowd of people threatening to come near him with sorrow in their eyes and sadness in their voices. He walked aimlessly about the memorial park, but instinctively headed to Jason's gravesite. He'd come here multiple times and knew the exact location where his partner was now buried.

When he came to the headstone, Ethan stared, recalling all memories of Jason, relishing most and banning the rest away. Things had never been the same between them after the debacle of the Johnson case. The hours they worked on that case to make sure the charges against Vanessa Johnson stuck went up in smoke the moment she aired out her and Jason's dirty laundry. Still, his guilt ate at him as he thought about that last night he'd seen Jason alive. It was the reason he kept coming back to this gravesite. He had to tell Jason he was sorry. He was sorry for leaving him alone and vulnerable to a murderer. Most of all, he was sorry for loving a woman that no longer belonged to him.

Then his thoughts shifted to the weeks after the trial. Jason had been suspended pending an investigation and Ethan petitioned for a new partner. For weeks, he'd dodged reporter's calls, took on new cases, and did whatever he could to return life back to normal. But not a month after the trial ended, Jason was killed, he'd become the number one suspect in his murder, and his life went into a tailspin. Then Angela came to town and offered to buy him a drink.

* * *

Three months earlier…

He still wasn't sure why he'd agreed to this. In fact, the longer he sat here waiting for her, he knew he should've just said no. He'd heard from Sophie that Angela had become a reporter and that she was in the process of moving to San Francisco from L.A. He was certain the news about the trial had made its way to southern California. Was she looking him up just to catch up with an old friend or was she looking for dirt?

Whatever she was up to, he decided he would indulge her a little only because Larry James had given him odd jobs to do while he was growing up. Sophie and Angela's father always treated him with respect, and like a man—not some poor white kid. Ethan's mom became a single mother when she divorced his dad when he was a baby. She never went after him for child support and according to her, he didn't have two nickels to rub together to even hint at alimony. As a result, things were tight around the house, but Mr. James never looked down on him or his mother. His first wife, Jennifer, before she died, taught Ethan's mother basic typing and computer skills, which landed her an office job down-town and gave them a better income. Yes, the James family had been good to him and his mother, which was why he'd always resisted the attraction he felt for his twin girls, Angela and Sophia, or the African-American versions of Betty and Veronica, as he'd always liked to call them, because even though they shared the same face, their personality differ-ences shone through. Plus, a day never went by when either one or both of them wasn't reading the Archie comics. They had a knack for knowing how to impersonate one another, and he had fallen victim to their little hoaxes more times than he could count. By the time he realized he was talking to Sophie when he thought he was talking to Angela, well...that was when he also realized the joke was on him. Still, he always prided himself in keeping his relationship with the girls as innocent as possible—a big brother to his younger sisters. They were attractive with their shared coffee-colored eyes and midnight hair, but beyond the physical traits, one of them had stood out, and she was beautiful inside and out to him. It had been hell trying to resist her, and one night on July 4, 2002, he stopped trying.

"What are you thinking about?"

He looked up to see Angela standing beside the barstool with a wide, radiant smile. He found himself smiling back, glad to see a friendly face after so much had happened in the past month.

"It's good to see you," he said, standing to give her a hug.

She returned his embrace, and then after a moment, stepped back to look at him. "It's good to see you too, Archie."

He laughed, gesturing to the barstool next to him. "I was just thinking about growing up with you two across the street from me and the nicknames we gave each other. What are you having?"

"Stoli on the rocks." She put her purse down on the bar and slid down on the stool. "Those were good times. It's a pity people have to grow up."

He signaled to the bartender and ordered her drink. Then he turned to her and conducted his own examination. She and Sophie must have been living similar lives, because he couldn't tell much difference between the two of them. Same killer, curvy figure, same length in hair...

"Still looking for differences, aren't you?" she asked and thanked the bartender when he brought her drink. She took a sip and then turned in her seat with a cocky smile. "We're identical, Ethan. Give it up."

"There's always some difference."

"And you've spent your whole life looking," she said, keeping that smile in place. "Give those cop's eyes a rest. Drink up and tell me what you've been up to for the past twenty years."

He scoffed. "You have that much time?"

"I have all the time in the world for you, now that I'll be traveling back and forth from here to L.A."

"I heard about that. When did you decide to make the move?"

"Shortly after Jason's funeral. Besides the fact that he was my brother-in-law, the case interested me, and I got approval from my boss to look into things more closely."

"What are you looking for?"

"His killer, of course."

"You mean you don't think it was me?"

She drummed her fingers lightly on the bar. "No, Ethan. I really don't think it was you. But if I'm going to help you, I'll need proof. You're going to need to learn to trust me and be willing to confide in me. Just like you used to."

They shared a meaningful look, rife with memories and everything she didn't say. And like always, whenever he thought of the past, one name came to the forefront of his mind.

"Is Sophie all right?"

Angela smiled, as if she expected him to bring her up. "She seems to be handling things well. You could just call her and ask her yourself."

He shook his head. "She doesn't want to talk to me. I tried to get her alone at Jason's funeral, but she avoided me."

Angela stared as if waiting for him to expound.

"It's a long story. Will you just tell her I asked about her?"

"How are you coping?" she asked. "You and Jason were partners, right?"

Ethan simply shrugged as though that said it all.

"I hear the investigation into his murder has gone cold. No suspects?"

He flagged down the bartender to give them both another refill on their drinks. "I can't tell if you're asking as an old friend or as a reporter."

"Sometimes the lines get blurred."

"I'll tell you what. I'll give you a little bit of detail about the case if you tell me Sophie is okay."

She studied him for so long that he began to wonder if maybe he'd offended her. It was pretty shitty of him to accept a woman's invitation to drinks but spend the time asking after another woman. But before Ethan could apologize, Angela began to smile and nodded her head as though she finally understood something.

"Deal." Then she winked, lifted her newly-filled glass and clinked it with his. "You use me. I use you."

CHAPTER ELEVEN

hree months earlier…
"Hello?"

"Hi, Angie. It's Ethan."

Pause.

"I know. I recognize your number. How are you?"

"I'm good. I was calling to thank you for meeting me the other night for drinks. It was nice to get together and talk about old times."

"I enjoyed it too."

Pause.

"I was also calling to see if you had a chance to talk to your sister."

"No, I haven't, but I will. You should just give her some time. She'll come around."

"I know. It's just that I need to talk to her about something. Something I saw…"

Pause.

"Ethan?"

"Yeah. Sorry. I was just thinking."

"You know, you could tell me what it is. I'm always happy to pass on the message."

"It's personal, Angie."

"I'm not going to put it on page one of the Chronicle. *I promise."*

Ethan laughed. "I know. Still, it would be nice to hear from her."

"I'll talk to her."

"Thanks."

"Ethan?"

"Yeah?"

"You know, I meant what I said at the bar that night. You can talk to me any time. You just need to trust me."

"I may just take you up on that. Good night."

"Good night."

***

Sophie had to endure more condolences at the wake her father and stepmother held at their home in Angela's honor. She accepted the hugs, hand grasping, and light kisses that went with those condolences, all the while surreptitiously looking at her watch. She couldn't help her sister here. So, as soon as it was acceptable, she kissed her father and Cynthia goodbye and made the trek from Hayward across the bridge and back into the city.

Angela's new place was in the Western Addition, a part of the city currently going through gentrification. There was a seal on her front door, which Sophie anticipated, but she also knew there was a broken latch on the window that entered into her bathroom. She told Angela many times to get it fixed, but she always said she was too busy. Now, Sophie was glad for it. She looked around the back alley to ensure she wasn't being watched and then lifted her body up and over the window frame. With the window tilted open, she slid inside the quiet bathroom now growing dark from the setting sun. She didn't have the foresight to change clothes but couldn't worry too much about the dust and smudges now staining her black dress or any runs in her pantyhose. Her heels were the only sound heard as she made her way from the bathroom into the hallway. The first room she came to was Angela's bedroom. There, she paused at the closed door, her hand hesitating on the doorknob. She knew on the other side of this door would be remnants of her sister's life, evidence that she had once lived. She backed away from the door and instead, went to the office. This door was open, and the first thing she spotted was the desk where Angela normally kept her laptop. But the laptop was gone.

"Damn," she said, opening the door wider, but not surprised at all. The police had made their sweep of the place for evidence.

Sophie crossed to the desk and rifled through papers, opened and closed file drawers, but without the laptop, she knew she was wasting her time. Angela wouldn't have left a print version of her story or notes lying around, waiting for someone to find them. Something as explosive as she claimed this to be would have been hidden very well.

She backtracked out of the office into the living and dining area. Aside from the stacks of books sitting in the corner, the area was both clean and tidy. Even being Angela's twin, she couldn't begin to guess her hiding places. She thought about trying her office at work but knew Hailey Cross and the gang would've confiscated everything there, too.

She paused in her search of the living room, moved to the sofa and sat down to think. She was convinced the story was the key to everything. If she could get her hands on it, Sophie had no doubt she'd find her sister's murderer, too. Then she realized something else. Maybe she didn't need to find the article at all, because someone out there knew what it was about. Someone living. She needed to find Angela's source.

A noise at the back of the house startled her and she instantly stood.

"Hello?"

Silence followed, but she knew she heard something.

"Is someone there?"

A shadow passed in the doorway of the bathroom and just as she thought to grab for the mace in her purse, the shadow moved into the living area and revealed a tall, broad, and imposing figure.

"What are you doing in here?"

His low, deep voice sounded almost like a growl, but the fear that raced up her spine only seconds ago was quickly replaced by relief and followed by indignation.

"Are you following me?"

Ethan stepped forward, now fully in the living area, and his presence seemed to make the space smaller.

"I asked you a question," he countered. "What are you doing in here? This property is sealed."

"I wanted to get away from the condolences, so I left my dad's house early. I didn't want to go home, yet, so I came here. I just wanted to be with her a bit longer."

It was partly the truth, but she could tell by the look on his face that he knew she was holding something back.

He stepped a little closer. "Why didn't you tell Cross and Sayres that I came to see you that afternoon?"

"I didn't think it was relevant. Besides, they were only concerned about the meeting Angie and I were supposed to have at the hotel."

"And what was this meeting about?"

"Just like I told them, I don't know.'"

"Now tell me the truth."

She narrowed her eyes in accusation. "You're calling me a liar, Ethan."

"Because you're lying to me. You know why she needed to meet with you. It's the reason you're here in this apartment. It's the reason it took you so long to open that hotel door."

"I have no idea what you're talking about. Like I said, I just wanted to be in Angie's presence for a while."

He seemed to relent and let her have that. For a few moments, he looked around the small space surrounding them, and then just as quickly, tossed another question at her.

"Why were you in the hotel room for so long?"

On reflex, she backed up and the front of the couch hit the back of her knees. Its touch and his question both surprised her and her reply came out sounding panicked.

"What?"

He didn't repeat it but continued to stare her down.

"Angie's hotel room?" She shrugged. "I'm not sure what you mean. When I found her body, I called you, then waited out in the living area for you. I was afraid to be near her, seeing her like that."

"I banged on that door over and over, but I could still hear you inside the room. Furniture was moving, drawers were being opened and closed." He paused to fix his eyes hard on hers. "You were looking for something. What was it?"

"I wasn't looking for anything."

He moved so close to her and tilted her chin upwards with his forefinger. She didn't know why she allowed him to touch her, but it felt so natural.

"When will you begin to trust me?" he asked, his tone low.

"I do trust you."

"That's a lie, and it's not the first one you've told me since we've been here. What were you looking for, Sophie?"

She couldn't look away from him if she'd wanted to. "The story. I was looking for the story."

"Why?"

She opened her mouth to speak, to tell him the truth, but something just wouldn't let her do it. She didn't know why she couldn't open up to him and just tell him she was looking for the story to destroy it. She didn't want him named as Jason's murderer. She didn't want it clear to her in bold black and white letters that her ex-lover from long ago killed her husband. That was not something she was ready to face.

Ethan's forefinger was still on her chin, keeping her head raised and looking at him. He was simply staring at her. She should be used to that look by now, having experienced the same stare from everyone she came into contact with that day, even her father. They were all looking for Angela, trying to see if her spirit remained in a woman who shared her face, but nothing else.

But Ethan's look lasted a bit longer than she was comfortable with, not only because of the gray tint his eyes held, but because he no longer seemed to be looking for Angela, but was actually staring at her, seeing Sophie. But if he saw Sophie, he was also seeing memories of a summer romance, stolen kisses, and more recently, forbidden moments.

"I only wanted to read it before it went to print."

"That's all?"

She nodded and stepped to the side, breaking his touch. He dropped his hand to his side and also moved away from her. And just like that, the moment for truth was gone.

"I could arrest you for being here, but I won't. Just leave, and don't come back until that seal is removed."

"Ethan—"

"Go home."

She didn't know what else to say, so she grabbed her purse and left the way she'd come in, refusing to let him see how much his dismissive tone hurt her. When she was once again outside, she took several deep breaths of the evening air, which now carried a chill. Being in such a small, enclosed space with Ethan wasn't good for her nerves. Before making her way down the street, she took one last look at the apartment. He was no doubt waiting for her to leave before he made his own exit.

Wrapping her jacket tightly around her, she clutched her purse and began walking back to her car, which was two streets over. But before she left the now darkened alleyway, she felt someone behind her. She thought it was Ethan, but before she could turn around, a gloved hand came over her mouth, and her back was shoved against the brick wall. She tried screaming, but the more she struggled, the tighter his hold became.

"Shut up! Shut the fuck up!"

She felt him jab something into her left side, and she instantly stilled.

"You feel that don't you?" he asked, his hot breath fanning her ear. "You make any more sudden moves, and it's over for you. I'll leave your dead body right here for the junkies to step over while they get their next hit. You got that?"

She nodded, now feeling tears warm her cold face.

"Tell me what the hell is going on. Those cops are looking for me. They want to question me about that night. Now you need to make things right and tell them I was only doing what you asked me. I turned off the video when your snitch came in the hotel. I did my part!"

Sophie couldn't keep the frown from showing on her face. Snitch? Then, a jolt of realization struck her, and she nearly stopped breathing.

He thinks I'm Angie.

"The papers said somebody was murdered in that room. I don't want anything to do with a fucking murder."

She shook her head slowly from left to right and splayed her hands in front of her to show him she wasn't going to run or scream if he would just let her talk. He turned her around, and she got a good look at his face. Brown eyes, even features, black curly hair, medium complexion. He looked familiar to her, and she thought maybe she had seen him in the lobby of the Franklin Hotel, but if she wanted answers, she had to keep him believing she was her sister.

She tried to speak as calmly and slowly as possible, even with tears flowing down her face.

"I'm sorry. I never meant to involve you in any way. I promise to make this right."

"You'd better. I've been hiding out in shitty motels, dodging cops for two weeks. You obviously got connections with them." He gritted his teeth, and his eyes turned deadly as he put the gun to her temple. "Tell them to back off."

"Okay." She raised her hands again in surrender. "I'll do it, just please put the gun away. Let's get out of here, so we can talk."

She needed to get him away from here, away from Ethan who could be coming out any moment. She needed to find out his name, but how did she get it without alerting him to who she really was?

"No, bitch. Just give me the money you promised me, and I'm out of here. You go talk to your cop friends while I get the hell out of this city."

Money? Her words faltered, and that was a mistake. He hit her on the side of the head with the butt of his gun, and she cried out, falling to the ground.

"Don't fuck with me," he said, standing over her. "Does two grand ring a bell? You think I'm playing with you?"

She wasn't looking up at him, too afraid he had that gun now pointed at her head. But the next sound she heard was the gun being knocked away to the ground. She looked up in time to see Ethan send his fist into the man's nose, and then came the sickening crack of cartilage and bone breaking. The man screamed in pain, and when he got his bearings, he turned his wrath on Ethan. He ducked his head and charged toward him, but Ethan had obviously guessed at his move and delivered a swift kick to the center of his forehead. The man's head snapped back and his eyes went into a daze before he fell to the ground, unconscious.

Ethan spared only a brief glance for the fallen man and then turned to help Sophie as she struggled to sit up while holding the side of her bleeding head.

He took hold of her elbow gently and pried her hand away from her head. "Let me see."

She let him examine the wound, which she could feel was already beginning to swell. Ethan cursed, took another look behind him to make sure the man was still unconscious, and then turned back to her.

"Can you walk?"

"I think so. My thigh is sore, but that's only because I hit the pavement so hard." She paused when she noticed him pulling out his cell phone. "What are you going to do?"

"Call it in," he said.

"Why?"

"I'm not on duty, and his ass is going to jail."

She struggled to keep her balance. "Let's just leave him. He can't hurt me now."

He ignored that but kept his eyes on her as he called dispatch and gave the necessary information. When he ended the call, he continued to stare at her.

"What did I interrupt here?" he asked. "A random mugging or something else?"

Sophie shrugged. "He wanted money. That's all I know."

He pulled a tissue from his jacket and stepped forward to place it over the wound on her head.

"Keep pressure there."

He held her hand in his a little longer than needed, and she risked looking back into his eyes. He met her stare.

"Was it the night Jason was killed? Was that when you stopped trusting me?"

"This is not the time, Ethan."

Was it the night I came to see you?"

She didn't answer.

"Please don't tell me it was that summer."

She nearly did speak then. She nearly told him it wasn't any of those times. She nearly said she never stopped trusting him. She just stopped trusting herself around him.

"What about me?" she asked. "Why did you never trust me as much as you trusted Angie?"

He opened his mouth to say something, but then she heard a groan, and they both turned to the man on the ground, who was slowly regaining consciousness.

* * *

Sophie was sitting in the ambulance, letting the EMTs stitch her head. An officer was there, ready to take her statement, and Ethan stood by listening as she recounted what happened.

"I remember sensing something wasn't right, but before I could do anything, he grabbed me from behind and pulled me into the alley."

"What did he say to you?"

She cut her eyes to Ethan. "He asked for my wallet and any jewelry I was wearing. I tried to push him away from me, and that's when he hit me."

The officer, a fit-looking black man in his early thirties, turned to Ethan. "Sergeant Markham, right?"

Ethan nodded.

"Looks like you were in the right place at the right time."

Ethan nodded and did his best to lie as close to the truth as possible. "Ms. James wanted to grab some personal things from her sister's apartment, but with the seal on the door, she couldn't enter. When she left, I realized it wasn't safe for her to be walking alone, so I went after her to see her to her car. I heard the struggle in the alleyway and saw the man hit her."

"And you hit him?"

"That's right."

"You broke his nose, Sergeant."

"I'll be sure to apologize the next time I see him beating up a woman in a dark alley."

The cop held up his hands as if to ward off Ethan's growing temper. "I'm not disagreeing with you. I've got a wife and two daughters at home, myself."

He turned back to Sophie. "I'm curious, Ms. James. Had you ever seen this man before?"

"No," Sophie said.

Ethan was absolutely sure she was lying. But why?

"Who is he?" Ethan asked.

"We ID'd him as Joshua Carelli. There's a BOLO out for him. He's wanted for questioning in Angela James's murder."

Ethan whipped his head in Sophie's direction, but she only looked away.

"It's a very strange coincidence that he's a person of interest in your sister's murder, and now he attacks you in an alley," the officer said, addressing Sophie again. "Are you certain you've never seen this man before?"

"I'm certain," she said with finality.

The officer then shared a brief look with Ethan, sighed heavily, and closed his notepad. "All right. I think I have everything I need. When you're ready, come down to make an official statement."

Sophie nodded. "Thank you, Officer."

"Sergeant," he said, nodding to Ethan.

As soon as he left, Ethan turned to her. "Does your father still live in Hayward?"

"Yes, but that's out of your way. You can just take me home."

"No. I want you to stay with someone you can trust. You've had a long day, and you're going to need to make a statement in the morning."

He looked at his watch. The drive across the bay to Hayward would take just over half an hour. It would give him just enough alone time with her to find out what Josh Carelli meant to her.

CHAPTER TWELVE

As soon as Ethan and Sophie entered the foyer of her father's home, he was hit with the aroma of roast chicken, and he realized he hadn't eaten anything since breakfast.

"Come in, both of you," Cynthia, Larry's wife, said, ushering them into the living area. She then took Sophie into her arms. "Are you all right?"

Cynthia James was a curvaceous woman of medium height. Her round face, bright eyes, and apparent laugh lines bespoke of a truly happy woman. Larry James, however, was her opposite with his hard-lined jaw, graying temples, and consistently stern expression. If Ethan hadn't known him since childhood, he would have thought he was an intimidating jerk.

Still, seeing the way he glared at his daughter as she came into the house, Ethan guessed his thoughts might be a little too mild.

"I can't believe someone just attacked you like that." Cynthia was cooing over Sophie, barely touching the bruise along the side of her head. "Are you in a lot of pain?"

"I'll be fine," Sophie promised. "I just need some fresh ice. This pack is growing warm."

"Give me just a second." Cynthia rushed away to the kitchen, but Ethan didn't miss the warning look she sent her husband's way. He was sure she was silently telling him to be nice and comfort his only living child.

But knowing Mr. James, Ethan knew the twin he favored the most, and in that respect, he always felt sorry for Sophie, even though she was constantly getting herself into trouble. He wondered now if her teenage antics were all to get her father to look at her the way he'd looked at Angela.

"Angela the Angel," he once heard Sophie mockingly say.

Larry's voice broke into Ethan's thoughts. "Didn't I tell you to carry your mace whenever you went out alone?"

"Oh, give me a break, Dad," was all Sophie said.

Ethan cleared his throat. "I need to be getting back to town. Get some rest. Someone will be contacting you tomorrow to come down to the precinct, make an official statement and ID the man."

Sophie was heading toward the kitchen after Cynthia and then stopped and turned at his words. She was giving him a wary look, and he knew she was remembering their conversation in Angela's apartment and again in the alleyway. No, it was probably not the right time to bring up their history, but when would be a good time? When she was dodging his phone calls or telling her assistant to tell him she was out when she was most likely hiding in her office? This was the first time since Jason's death that he'd been able to get her alone. He wanted to talk to her about that night. He didn't want her listening to accounts from Internal Affairs, but he wanted her to hear what he had to say. He wanted to tell her he wasn't going to reveal everything about the night he saw Jason. He wanted to ease her fears.

As soon as he'd had her alone in the car, he barely hinted

at the subject, and she quickly shut him down. He had to admit to himself that Sophie was never going to want to revisit that night. But in the meantime, he was still a suspect.

"Thank you, Ethan, for looking after her." Larry extended his hand, to which Ethan accepted. "Have you had dinner? There's plenty of leftovers from the wake. You should have something before heading back to the city."

The offer was tempting, but what would be the point—only to stay in Sophie's company a while longer. She'd been tight-lipped the entire ride over here, and he couldn't browbeat her into telling him what the asshole was after. He felt a slight pang of guilt for having to leave her after what had happened, but she'd be safe here with her father and step-mother. Then he turned toward the door, opened it, and couldn't resist turning back for one last look at Sophie. She was still watching him. He would let her have her secrets. For now.

"Thank you, sir, but I made plans and need to get back." After saying his goodbyes and making promises to not be a stranger, he turned to Sophie.

"Take care of yourself," he said and let himself out.

CHAPTER THIRTEEN

*E*ight months earlier…

The buzzer to the security door startled Ethan as he stirred his dinner over the stove that evening. He turned the heat down low and went to the intercom.

"Yeah?"

"It's me. Open up."

Ethan paused and then lowered his head and sighed.

"Come on, Ethan. Please."

After another slight hesitation, he pushed the button to open the security door for his guest. He then left the front door to his apartment slightly ajar and went back to stirring his food. In a few moments, he heard the door shut and the sound of footsteps slowly walking up behind him. Ethan turned just as Jason grabbed a seat on one of the bar stools.

"There's fucking press outside my house. Their news vans are parked up and down the block. I needed somewhere quiet to go, and it looks like you're not as popular as me."

Ethan grunted turned back around to pour the pasta into a strainer, and reached under the cabinet to grab the olive oil. The silence stretched between them before Jason spoke again.

"If I wanted to be ignored, I could go back home to Sophie."

Ethan mixed the oil into the spaghetti. "I'm doing you a favor. Don't expect me to like it."

He heard him sigh. "I know you're angry at me and disappointed Hell, everybody is. The Lieutenant put me on administrative leave while my conduct is being investigated —their words."

Ethan opened the refrigerator, reached in to grab two bottles of beer, and turned to hand one to Jason. "What did you expect them to do? They need to protect the department."

Jason shrugged as he took the bottle opener Ethan offered him and uncapped his beer. "I don't know what I was expecting. I mean, I knew there would be a shitstorm when this all came out, which is why I asked her not to do it."

Ethan took a swig of beer and then scoffed. "Did you really think she wasn't going to try and save her own ass?"

"I don't know, dammit!"

"You had an affair with the defendant. The key suspect in our case. Just tell me one thing. Were you two fucking before or after we arrested her for poisoning her stepson?"

"Before."

"All that time, while interviewing witnesses, during her arrest, during her questioning, you didn't say anything?" Ethan slammed his bottle down on the countertop. "Just interrogating that woman was enough to give her a mistrial."

Jason clasped the beer bottle between his hands. "I wasn't thinking. I knew I should have ended it with her a long time ago to save my marriage and career. She was bad for me in all possible ways. Then, when I found out she was under investigation for what she did to that little boy, I did try to break it off. But she threatened to tell everyone about us. Little did I know, she planned to do it anyway."

He slammed his fist on the counter. "Look, I'm a fucking idiot, all right? Nobody knows that more than me. I don't know what's going to come of all of this, and I don't want to know. At least not now. Can we talk about something else?"

"Sure," Ethan said, feeling the features on his face go as rigid as stone. "Let's talk about your wife."

Jason's eyes narrowed in anger at Ethan, and then he shook his head and chuckled. "If you want to know the truth, Sophie is the least of my problems."

"How's that?"

Jason angled his head to the pot of spaghetti. "Did you make more than enough for one? I'm starving."

Ethan regarded him for a moment and then turned and grabbed two plates from one of the upper cabinets. He put a heaping amount of pasta and meat sauce on one and handed it to Jason before preparing his own plate.

Jason wound his fork in the spaghetti and let out a long sigh. "Our marriage isn't what you'd expect. I know she loves and cares for me, but she knew what kind of man I was before she married me."

Ethan paused, the bottle of his beer right at his lips. "That's bullshit. You're telling me she didn't expect you to stay faithful? The Sophie I know…"

Realizing what he was about to say, he let the rest of his words go, but not soon enough. Jason's eyes slowly moved from his plate to meet Ethan's dead on.

"What do you know about her?"

Ethan chose his words carefully. He knew she hadn't told Jason about their history, and it wasn't his place to let that secret out.

"She doesn't strike me as the kind of woman who would tolerate a cheating husband."

Jason's eyes never wavered, and they only seemed to harden. "Then I guess you don't know shit, do you partner?"

CHAPTER FOURTEEN

"Were you fired?"

Sophie was very proud of herself for not letting her fork clang to the dinner plate in exasperation and openly rolling her eyes at her father. She had not forgotten the childhood lesson to respect one's elders, although her father seemed to love putting her to the test each time she was in his presence.

Still, she paused with her fork halfway to her lips and looked up at him. "No, Dad. I told you, my boss gave me a temporary leave of absence. It's only until this whole thing with Angela blows over."

He harrumphed. "Your sister's death isn't just going to blow over, Sophia."

"She didn't mean it that way, Larry."

Sophie looked to Cynthia with gratitude. Although, she'd been married to her father for years, Sophie didn't think of the woman as only her stepmother, but that of an older friend. She seemed to make her father happy, which was all Sophie cared about. She was also good to have around on nights like this to serve as a buffer between Sophie and her father.

Even now, her father's eyes seemed to soften when he looked at his wife. "I'm just tired of everyone, the news media especially, treating her death as if it were the sensation of the week. She was a human being."

"You and I know that. Sophie knows that, too," Cynthia continued softly. "That's all that matters." She paused as a smile crossed her features. "Your sister came to visit us last week. It was such a nice surprise."

Sophie frowned. "She did?"

Cynthia nodded. "She was so excited about some story she was working on. She couldn't give us specifics, but she kept saying 'I'm so close, Dad. I'm so close.' Didn't she, honey?"

My dad was slower to nod. "She kept saying how huge this story was and that it was going to make her career. She was practically lifting this dinner table with her excitement."

He stopped to look at the empty chair across from me, which had always been Angela's seat, and Sophie pretended to not notice the sheen in his eyes.

She cleared her throat. "I'm glad you two got to see her, before…before everything."

"She even spent the night and went to breakfast with us in the morning," Cynthia said.

Larry nodded in agreement, sighed heavily, and then turned back to her. "Tell me what happened tonight."

Cynthia clucked her tongue. "For Christ's sake, let the girl finish eating."

"No, it's fine," Sophie said. "I'd rather talk about it now that I've got my energy back and while it's still fresh in my mind."

So she told them about her impromptu visit to Angela's place, giving them the same reason she gave Ethan. She didn't know if they knew that Angela was planning on accusing a cop within the SFPD of murder and decided to keep that news to herself.

"I know it was stupid and foolish, but I wanted to help find her killer. I figured the best place to start looking would be her apartment."

She continued on explaining how she left the apartment and was attacked and pulled into an alley by a mugger—not by someone who thought she was Angela.

"I don't ordinarily carry a lot of cash, so when he looked in my bag and found only twenty bucks, he didn't believe me when I told him that's all I had."

"And he hit you?" Cynthia asked, holding her hand to her mouth.

Sophie nodded. "Yeah, he hit me."

She dared a glance at her father and was surprised to find him staring at her with a mixture of concern and anger. She could guess at the concern, but was the anger for the fact that his daughter was attacked on the same day his other daughter was buried? Or did he suspect she wasn't being entirely truthful with them?

Then his expression turned blank as he nodded at her plate. "Finished with that?"

She looked down at the barely eaten roast chicken and vegetables and realized she wasn't as hungry as she'd thought. "Yes. I'm sorry to waste it, Cynthia. It was delicious."

"Don't trouble yourself," Cynthia said, getting up from the table to collect the dishes. "After the day you've had, I'm surprised you could barely keep your head from falling into the plate."

Sophie took that as her opening. "I guess it's now hitting me how tired I am. If you don't mind, I'll head up to bed."

"Goodnight," came Cynthia's warm reply.

Her father cleared his throat. "Cindy changed the bed

sheets when we heard you were coming. You know where your old bedroom is."

Sophie smiled her thanks at her stepmother and tossed a muttered goodnight to her father before heading up to the room she and Angela shared as young girls.

* * *

She found an old T-shirt and shorts in the bureau drawer and figured they would do as pajamas for the night. After she'd used the bathroom to scrub her face clean and tied her hair into one single braid, she went back into her bedroom, sat on the double bed by the window, which had been hers, and stared at her sister's bed against the wall.

The thought that she would no longer be able to pick up the phone and speak to her brought such a wrenching pain in the pit of Sophie's stomach. Then she remembered that she and Angela hardly ever spoke on the phone, except when it came to their father or a favor Angela wanted from her. In truth, Sophie had spoken to Angela more times in this past year than in the three years since Angela moved to L.A. She'd never thought about it much. They were both busy, professional women, looking to make a name for themselves in their respective careers. Surely, a lack of conversation could be forgiven. But that wrenching pain in her stomach told Sophie it couldn't be forgiven, because her twin sister's bed would go undisturbed, and there was nothing she could do about it. All she had left were the memories of the two of them as girls sitting in this very room, giggling about a boy one of them had a crush on, a close friend who wore a hideous skirt to school that day, or a teacher who was just too boring for words. And sometimes, they wouldn't say anything but pass secrets to one another on folded colored paper, leaving the notes under one another's mattress.

Mom will be asleep around nine. Cover for me.

Dad thinks I'm studying at Tasha's. I'll be with Mike if you need me.

I got a D in Algebra. If you see my report card, hide it.

Sophie smiled at their little game, remembering how Angela came up with the idea to use the password *Archie* to let the other one know a secret was waiting under the mattress. They both loved the Archie digest comics and giggled over Ethan's habit of referring to Angela as Betty and Sophie as Veronica. Surprisingly, the password system worked for years until they were old enough to leave their parents' home, taking their secrets with them and leaving their innocence behind.

"Sophie?"

She jumped slightly and saw her father standing in the doorway.

"Dad, you scared me," she said on a breath.

He took one hesitant step into the room. "I, uh, thought that if you were uncomfortable with sleeping here, you could take the guest room."

She was touched and a little surprised by his concern but shook her head. "It's all right. I'll be fine here tonight."

She thought he'd turn and leave after that, but he looked as though he wanted to say more. She waited him out, knowing this private moment between them wouldn't happen again for a long time.

"What's this leave of absence really for?" he asked.

She frowned. "I told you. My boss wants me to take some time until Angie's murder is solved."

"What does that have to do with whether you work or not?"

She sighed. Earlier, she'd breezed over this topic, believing her father and Cynthia would think it a moot point considering she'd been mugged. But her father had been there since childhood and knew all her tricks.

"It's not a big deal, but the officers investigating the case have been to my office a couple of times. You and I were busy planning the funeral and getting Angie's estate in order, so there were several days I wasn't there to see them."

"They were asking questions about you?"

She nodded.

He put his hands to his hips, looked to the ceiling, and mouthed a few words she couldn't decipher, but from the look on his face when he focused again on her, she knew they weren't very nice words.

"Are you telling me you're a suspect in your own sister's murder?"

She rushed to calm the situation before his temper exploded. She remembered that look of his from when Angela and her were girls, and it meant he was reaching his breaking point.

"I was the one who found her. Listen, I've worked on murder cases before. This is how it's done. They suspect everyone, ask questions about everyone and eliminate people. We're in the early stages of this investigation, and right now, everyone's a suspect."

"They haven't come knocking on my door, Sophie."

"You've got an alibi, Dad. You and Cynthia were here all night."

He still looked ready to chew nails. However, she couldn't decide whether he was mad at the cops for suspecting her, or at her for somehow getting herself into this whole mess. Knowing her father, it was probably a bit of both.

"What about Ethan?" he asked. "Is he a suspect too? They suspected him of killing Jason. Do you believe them?"

"I don't know. Can we just deal with one thing at a time?

Like I said, this is all a matter of routine. Think of it as a process of elimination."

His eyes hardened. "Don't talk down to me like those 'stick-up-the-ass' lawyer friends of yours. I'm not stupid."

Here we go, she thought. "I wasn't talking down to you. I just don't want you to get excited about something when there isn't any need to."

"What about Jason? He was a reason to get excited, wasn't he?"

"I'm not talking about Jason, Dad."

"But I am. You told me to calm down about him, too, and look what happened? He humiliated you for everyone to see, and you know what? I wasn't surprised. I knew what kind of man you married long before he showed his true colors to you."

"And that's a reason to turn your back on me?"

"You stopped coming to me!"

He paused, took a few breaths, and continued on in a lower tone, but Sophie could still hear the hurt in his voice.

"After your mother died, you girls came to me for everything. It was scary as hell at first, having to raise two teenagers with emotions that only a mother could understand and questions that only a mother could answer. But I got the hang of it, and I began to love that you girls trusted me enough to come to me with all of your problems—even when you were grown women and had left the house."

"Dad," Sophie started but didn't know what she wanted to say.

"I know a daughter is supposed to leave and make her own family with a strong man, but he wasn't what I had in mind for you, and I was hoping that one day you'd see that and come to me. I was waiting for you, Sophie."

He took a deep breath and for the first time, looked about the room. His gaze swept over all the paraphernalia typical of two teenage girls. He stopped at Angela's side of the room with her double bed and pastel green duvet, contrary to Sophie's pale blue covering.

She followed his gaze and studied her sister's shelves over her bed. Softball and volleyball trophies, old school textbooks, pictures taken with high school friends, her burgundy graduation cap and yellow tassel. A lump rose in Sophie's throat, knowing her side of the room was almost a mirror image. Then she looked to her Dad and wished she had the courage to get up from the bed, go to him, and put her arms around him. But she didn't have the courage, and neither did he.

He turned to her and gave a brusque nod, followed by a too formal goodnight. After he closed the door behind him, she got into her bed, turned off the lamp, and lay under her covers looking through the window to the moon. Then a thought came to her, and she realized what she had to do. Even with all the department's support, Jason's case had grown cold due to lack of evidence. But in Angela's case, there was still time to get to the truth.

She flung the covers away and grabbed her cell phone by the bed. She scrolled through her contacts and walked to the window as she listened to the other end ring. Looking down on the street, she was surprised to see Ethan's car, still parked in its same spot by the curb. He was supposed to have left a while ago, but something was keeping him here. The other line picked up, and she kept her eyes on Ethan's car as she spoke.

"Hi, Wayne. This is Sophie. I need you to look up a man in holding for me. Joshua Carelli."

Once she relayed to her colleague the instructions she needed him to carry out for her, she ended the call but continued staring down at Ethan's car. She knew he was looking up at her, but she didn't wave or make any other kind of gesture. After a moment, she moved away from the window and to the vanity Angela and she used to share. Turning around, she lifted her pajama top and eyed the faint scar that lined her lower left back. With it, came a cloud of memories that never seemed to be too far from her mind. But rather then succumb and let them fill her up with visions of what might've been, she lowered her shirt, climbed into bed, and switched off the light.

CHAPTER FIFTEEN

*E*than sat in his car, reviewing the images on his cell phone as he had done every night since Angela's murder. He was looking for something, anything that could explain what had happened that night. But like the numerous times before, he saw nothing and no one suspicious except for one person. And seeing that one person always made him want to punch the wall. How could he have been so stupid? Why couldn't he have just let things go? Conveniently, the images stopped after that. There was nothing else to see, and he knew if this ever got into Hailey or Noah's hands, he was fucked.

He put the phone away and looked up at the now still and silent house of Larry and Cynthia James. He'd lied when he said he had plans. After the front door closed behind him, he'd gotten in his car and stayed there, watching the house. Call it instinct, but he didn't want to leave her alone just yet. Yes, she had her family with her, but he'd seen the look in her eyes before he turned away. She was scared of something, and the last time he'd seen fear in her eyes was the night Jason died. Now, having seen that look again, it had taken every ounce of strength in him not to draw her into his arms and tell her everything would be all right. But ever since the night Jason found them in the kitchen together, Sophie would not allow Ethan to touch her. Judging from this afternoon, he could see it still made her nervous to be alone with him. But God forgive him, he couldn't stop thinking about how good she'd felt in his arms—how right. In the next moment, guilt assailed him just as it always did when he thought about her, that night, and what might have happened. He was on his way out of the house. He was going to leave, but if Jason hadn't come home when he did…

Ethan let those thoughts go, now ashamed of himself. She had been a married woman at the time, and he had no right to touch her. He knew that. But the selfish side of him, the raw and carnal side of him, wouldn't stop insisting and reminding him that Sophie had belonged to him first. That summer, she had been completely his.

"I didn't think you liked me," she said. "I didn't even think you noticed me beyond Angie's twin sister."

"I noticed. I've always liked you. But you were a good girl and out of respect for your dad, I left you alone."

"And now?" she asked.

He took a moment to calm his loins and tried to remember that this was Sophie James. She was the daughter of a man who had been good to him and his mother. He used to see her and Angela like little sisters who always seemed to giggle stupidly around him. Yes, she was still Sophie. She was still a good girl. But she had grown into a beautiful woman, and he wanted her.

"Now," he said, pausing to tuck a strand of her hair behind her ear, "we're both over eighteen, and this is the first time we've ever been alone without your parents, my mother or your sister around. I'm glad you kissed me."

Afterwards, he'd asked her out, and the look on her face made him wonder if she thought she was just going to be a one-night stand. He wanted to tell her she couldn't be any further from the truth.

"I want to see you again," he said.

"You do?"

Yes, he did. Besides working, it seemed like all he did that summer was see her every chance he could get. He was lost in her.

Soft light illuminated from the upstairs bedroom, chasing away the memory, and a silhouette of a woman came to the window. Sophie. He remembered that her and Angela's room was in the front of the house, facing the street. She pulled back the curtains and he knew with certainty she'd seen him. But he didn't drive away or try to hide in the darkness. He simply stared up at her, just as boldly as she was staring down at him. He wanted her to see him, wanted her to know he was there and hoped she found some comfort in that.

Finally, she closed the drapes and her shadow disappeared from the window. She would be safe for the rest of the night. He looked at his watch and then turned on his ignition and pulled into the street. Carelli would have been processed and put in holding by now. He was anxious to see just what the kid had to say for himself.

ailey was watching television when her work phone rang. Her shift had ended nearly two hours ago, and after a dinner of two slices of cold leftover pizza and a glass of wine, she resigned to end the day on her couch, flipping through sitcom reruns.

When her cell continued to ring on the table next to the sofa, she eyed it for a moment and sighed long and heavy before reaching over, switching on the lamp, and answering the call.

"Cross."

"We found Josh Carelli," Noah stated without preamble.

Hailey fell silent, and he must have mistaken her silence for confusion because he began to explain.

"The missing employee at the Franklin Hotel."

"Yes, I remember." Hailey picked up the TV remote and muted the program. "Where is he?"

"In holding. It looks like he fell right into our laps."

She immediately stood, eyeing her purse and jacket on a hook by the door. "I'm on my way. What's he in lockup for?"

"Assault, and that's where it gets interesting," Noah said.

"The arresting officer ran his name and found out he's wanted for questioning in Angela James's murder and called me."

"So?" Hailey held the phone to her ear as she shrugged on her jacket. "Have his victim ID him, and he's ours to question."

"Hailey," Noah said and then paused. "His victim is Sophia James."

She stopped just as her hand reached the doorknob, and her purse fell from her hands to the floor. "Sophia James? What? Why?"

"Just get here as soon as you can."

He hung up without another word. Hailey clutched the phone in her hand, walked stiffly back to her couch, and plopped down. As if in a daze, she stared at the actors on the television screen doing what they did best to make the audience laugh, and the very sight of happiness and jocular moods suddenly offended her. In one motion, she swept away all the contents of the coffee table and watched in satisfaction as everything crashed to the floor.

* * *

Ethan knew Carelli would be taken to the downtown holding facility and chose to meet them there. Just as he'd suspected, Cross and Sayres were called down to question Carelli about his disappearance from the Franklin Hotel the night Angela was killed. Ethan, himself, was curious to hear his explanation, as well as why he attacked Sophie tonight. He didn't believe Sophie's story that the man had just been a random mugger—especially not after he'd been identified and the officer revealed his connection to Angela's murder. He'd said something to Sophie in that alleyway, and if he couldn't get the answers from her, he was sure to get Carelli to open his mouth in exchange for a plea deal. Ethan hoped either Hailey or Noah would be in an accommodating mood and allow him to observe the interview just as he did when they interviewed Sophie.

But the moment Noah spotted him, he nudged Hailey, and Ethan could tell he mouthed the words: *What the fuck is he doing here?*

When Hailey turned to see who her partner was referring to, she looked both surprised and disappointed, but Ethan ignored all of that and strode toward both of them. Without missing a beat, he started in on his demands.

"I want to be in the room."

Noah scoffed. "You're insane."

Hailey, always the more diplomatic one, shook her head. "I'm not letting you one inch near that kid until you tell me what you were doing with Sophia James in her dead sister's apartment."

"I want to know why he attacked her."

"There was a seal on that door," Noah said. "You're lucky Hailey likes you because if it was up to me, I'd have you in lockup right now for interfering in a criminal investigation."

Ethan barely spared him a glance. "One has nothing to do with the other."

Noah stepped forward. "I'm not so sure about that."

Hailey quickly stepped between the two of them and shot daggers at her partner. "Stop it!" Then she looked to Ethan. "He's right. You two didn't belong in that apartment and being there, you could have compromised an investigation."

"I got her out of there as soon as I could," Ethan said. "I only followed her out there, hoping she would tell me what she was looking for."

"You're not on this investigation, Markham," Noah said through gritted teeth.

Hailey held up a hand to silence him. "And did you find out what that something was?"

"The story Angela was supposedly working on before she was killed. It had to do with Jason's murder. Apparently, Angela had a source that named Jason's killer. Rumor has it that it was a cop and the department is covering it up."

"Yeah, we heard the rumors," Hailey said. "Internal Affairs is handling Jason's murder. If there was a cover up, they would have found it by now. Besides, the only person…"

She trailed off and looked away from Ethan in embarrassment.

"It's okay. You can say it," he said. "I was, and still am, their main suspect. My guess is, that source named me."

"What does she have to say about that?" Hailey asked, referring to Sophie.

"She told me the same thing she told you. She doesn't know who the source is."

"Do you believe her?" Hailey asked.

"I believe that if she doesn't know who murdered her husband, she knows something else. Just before I broke that thug's nose for slapping her around, I heard him demand money from her."

Hailey stared at him for a long time, and Ethan deduced she was trying to see what more he wasn't telling her. Then, she turned around and shared a look with Noah.

"What a fucking nightmare," she said under her breath and started to walk away.

"Hailey—" Ethan started to call after her.

She whirled around in anger, pointing a finger at him. "You're not going in that room with us. You're not even going to listen in. This is my and Noah's investigation. Do yourself a favor, get a lawyer and quit involving yourself."

"Get a lawyer?" Ethan walked up to her, and he could feel his own anger begin to rise. "Am I a suspect in this case, too?"

She didn't answer him but kept her eyes trained on him as she called to her partner. "Let's go, Noah. We need to interview Carelli."

"That won't be happening, Sergeant."

Ethan looked up to see a harried-looking man walking toward them with a thick manila folder clutched in his arms. He reached his free hand into his pocket and extracted a business card to hand to Hailey.

"I'm Wayne Dyer with the Public Defender's office."

Hailey didn't take the card. "Nice to meet you, Mr. Dyer, but I wasn't aware that Mr. Carelli asked to have an attorney present."

"He didn't. I'm only here to ensure his release is handled efficiently."

"His release?" Hailey nearly screeched the word.

For the first time, Ethan noticed two uniformed officers a few feet away from the public defender. They were heading inside the interview room where Carelli was waiting. One had his handcuff keys out.

"What the hell is going on?" Noah asked.

Wayne pocketed his business card. "Mr. Carelli is being released on the basis that all charges against him have been dropped."

Ethan dropped his head at the lawyer's words and prayed for strength. When he looked up, he saw that Josh Carelli was walking out of the interview room with a bruised and bandaged nose and no restraints. When he spotted Ethan, he gave him the middle finger. Ethan decided then that when he saw Sophie again, he may end up finishing the job this little punk started. What game was she trying to play?

"Wait a damn minute!" Hailey went after Josh and the officers as they began to lead him to requisitions where he would pick up his belongings. "He may not be under arrest, but I still need to interview him. He is wanted for questioning in a murder investigation."

"Talk to me when I have a lawyer, bitch," Carelli shouted over his shoulder and continued his stride.

"Have a good night." Wayne Dyer gave them an apologetic look and followed after Carelli and the officers.

Hailey stood, seething in the middle of the hallway, and Ethan prepared himself for her wrath. When she finally focused on him, the look she gave him would cut glass.

"I don't know what your little girlfriend is up to, but please tell her that the next time she interferes in my investigation, her husband's death won't be the only murder this department covers up."

"Watch it, Hailey," Ethan said, his body rigid. "You're talking recklessly right now."

"Can you blame me?" she erupted. "That little shithead who just walked out of here was there the night of her sister's murder and disappeared before we could talk to him. Tonight, you witness him beating her up in an alley, and what does she do? She drops the charges! Why Ethan?"

The moment she asked that question, silence fell again, only this time, it was laden with possibilities that Ethan didn't want to face. Why indeed? The first answer that came to his mind was too horrific and unbelievable, he didn't want to dwell on it. But when he looked at Hailey and Noah, they were looking back at him, and he could see in their eyes that their cop brains had fallen on the same thought.

"Could she have really—" Noah began and then stopped.

"I'm going home." Ethan turned and walked away from them. He needed to get somewhere quiet and think.

"You were right about her. She does know something," Hailey called after him. "I'm going to bring her back in, Ethan. Fair warning."

CHAPTER SEVENTEEN

*E*ight months earlier...

"Who is it?"

"Ethan."

There was a long pause on the other side of the door before he finally heard the lock click. Sophie slowly opened it, and Ethan noticed she was dressed in gray leggings and a sweater. Her hair was in a messy ponytail and her face was scrubbed clean of makeup, making her soft brown skin look years younger.

"Jason isn't here," she said by way of greeting.

"I know. I came to see you."

"I'm fine, and you really shouldn't have come."

She started to close the door, but he placed a firm hand on it to stop it from shutting in his face.

"Sophie please, let me say what I need to say, and I'll leave. I promise not to stay long."

Her eyes held his for a moment until she stepped back without a word and let him inside. Ethan stepped inside the foyer, shut the door, and followed her into the softly lit living area.

"I just put some water in the kettle. Tea will be ready in a few minutes, or I can make you some coffee."

"No, thank you. Look, I came because I wanted to apologize for—for everything."

She gave a nonchalant shrug and then gestured for him to sit down on the sofa while she chose the love seat opposite him.

"Those are the breaks, right?"

"No, don't do that. None of that should have happened. I should have known what was going on and—"

"And what?" she asked. "And stopped it? What could you have possibly done to prevent any of this? They were having an affair, and she used that relationship to get a mistrial. Honestly, if I were in her shoes, I'd probably do the same thing."

He let that go for the moment. "Where's Jason?"

"He found a weekly rental and moved out. I thought that was him at the door coming to get more of his things."

"Is there anything I can do?"

She cocked her head to the side and sent him a smile that was laced with sarcasm just as the kettle began to whistle. "No thanks. You've done enough."

She got up to go turn off the stove, and Ethan knew he should just use that moment to say goodnight and walk out of there. But his ego just couldn't let that go. He stood and went after her into the kitchen where she was pouring hot water into a mug.

"If there's something you want to say to me, Sophie, I'm right here. Just say it."

She slammed the kettle onto the stove with a loud clang but still didn't turn around. He did, however, notice her back stiffen as she dipped a tea bag in and out of the mug.

He ventured again. "I didn't know I would be meeting you that evening in the restaurant. Jason told me your name, but

I chalked it up to coincidence. Then when I saw you..." He paused and chose his words carefully before continuing. "I never would've petitioned to be his partner if I'd known you were his wife."

She turned, gripping the handle of the mug as her face flushed with anger. "What does it matter now, Ethan? I don't care if Jason knows that we used to date. I'm more concerned about why you didn't tell your partner that fucking the suspect is bad for his wife's case?"

"I told you I didn't know anything about it."

"He was your partner. He didn't share things with you?"

"He was your husband. He didn't share things with *you*?"

Her eyes went from angry to wounded, and he knew that remark cut deep.

"I'm sorry," he said, feeling shame wash over him. "That was out of line."

She held up a hand to stop him from apologizing any further. "What do you want from me?"

"I want you to yell at me, call me names, whatever you want, because I know you're furious. I am, too! Or did you not want to win this case as bad as I did?"

"Of course I wanted her put away. My job was snatched away from me, and I had to go back to the DA's office with my tail between my legs, begging my boss for my job back. Furious is mild compared to what I was feeling!"

He nodded. "Just like I thought, you had your head in the clouds from day one. I told you to be serious about it, but you were too focused on your new office space to worry about one measly conviction."

"Goddamn you," she shouted. "I wanted to see her rot for killing that little boy as much as anyone. It hurt like hell to see her walk away, but when I'd heard Carl Johnson put a bullet to her brain, I wanted to cheer. I wanted to defend him!" Her vehemence diminished as she lowered her head and spoke softly. "Then I'd heard he'd shot himself."

They both went silent, mourning the loss of an entire family because of one tragedy.

"You're right," Sophie said on a weary sigh. "I was excited about my new job. I knew that winning this case would make my career, but I did everything by the book, because a conviction would mean that Matthew got justice. You and I were both sidelined by Jason's lies. Now, that entire family is dead, Jason is suspended, and I don't know what I'm going to do about my career or my marriage or anything else."

She looked away and seemed to ponder her own words for a moment. Then she looked back at him. "What are you going to do?"

Ethan shrugged. "I've already put in the request for a new partner."

"Does Jason know?"

"I haven't told him yet. I was going to wait until his disciplinary hearing was over, but now I'm not so sure."

"Why?"

Instead of answering, he took a tentative step toward her. "You're going to stay with him, aren't you?"

"Ethan."

"Just tell me the truth. Tell me that is exactly what you plan to do, so that I can walk away from you and quit hoping for something that's never going to happen."

She was looking at him, and he could see in her eyes she was silently pleading for him to stop.

"I told you I don't know what I'm going to do."

"That night he introduced us. How do you think I felt, sitting across from the two of you?"

"I can't talk about this with you."

"I was having dinner with my partner while remembering the days and nights you and I had together."

The air seemed to still around them.

"That was so long ago, Ethan. It was just one summer."

"So that's it? That's all I get is one summer?"

"Yes. It ended there."

"That's not good enough."

He was upon her now, and he knew she saw what was in his eyes. However, she didn't back up. They met in the middle of the kitchen, and as he took hold of her arm, she tried to raise her hand to slap him. He stopped her hand in midair and took hold of her other arm. The mug of tea she was holding crashed to the floor and they began to struggle with each other.

"Stop it, Sophie!"

"I'm so angry with you," she shouted.

"I know."

"I hate him!"

"I know, and it's all right, but I'm not going to fight with you." He was grasping both of her arms and shaking her to get her attention. "I don't want to hurt you."

She stopped trying to hit him and allowed her body to go still. She looked up at him and he saw desperation in her eyes. "Then why did you come here? Why do you keep making me remember?"

They stood there together amid broken shards and spilled tea, and he knew she was sharing the same memory of the past and remembering how simple it had been. How it had just been the two of them. Before Jason.

He couldn't help it. The look she gave him sent him back to the innocent and vibrant woman she had been when she allowed him to have her. He had to kiss her. He had to keep remembering. He took her in his arms and his lips swept over her full mouth. She tasted so good, so familiar. Every curve and inch of her he'd tried to commit to memory years ago but couldn't hold onto. Now, he was reacquainting himself with her arms, waist, and hips. Sophie returned his kisses and roamed her hands up and down his back as though she were doing the same thing. Ethan moaned, backed her up against the cabinets, and lifted her onto the counter. She immediately spread her legs to allow him to stand between them, and the kiss turned even more intense, passionate—and forbidden.

Alarm bells sounded in his head, deafening him and quickly destroying the fantasy he was trying to create. This was wrong. Goddammit, this was wrong, and as their movements slowed, he knew they were both realizing it at the same time.

Ethan slowly ended the kiss, but kept his forehead resting against hers, allowing both of them to ease their breathing and let all desire fade away. He then began to back away, leaving Sophie staring after him in shock. He watched as she raised her fingers to her lips lightly grazing them, as if she could still feel him. He could certainly feel her.

"I should go."

She only nodded.

He looked around the floor at the spilled tea and porcelain shards from the broken mug. "If you get me a broom and mop, and I can clean this up before I go."

"No," she said, hopping down from the counter. I can handle it."

He couldn't stop staring at her. "I'm sorry. I never should have—that's not why I came here."

"I know," she said. "But please, Ethan. Just go."

The front door opened and then closed, startling them both. Ethan turned toward the sound, knowing who it was, and then back to Sophie and saw she was wearing the same guilty expression as himself.

CHAPTER EIGHTEEN

*E*arly the next morning, Sophie left her dad and stepmother a note, thanking them for letting her stay the night. She knew it was cowardly of her, but she didn't want to face her dad after the argument they'd had last night. She hired a car service to take her back to Angela's neighborhood to get her car, and then she went home and changed into jeans, a warm sweater, and sneakers and left minutes later to drive to the address Wayne was able to get for her while Carelli had been in holding.

The address he gave her was a low-budget motel on the border of the Tenderloin district. Sophie parked at the end of the block where she still had a clear view of the place and turned off the car engine. She didn't like having to wait in this neighborhood but needed a chance to speak with Josh privately, away from the police. If she'd pressed charges against him for attacking her, he would be in jail, and that wouldn't do at all. He thought she was Angela, and she was determined to get the answers she needed from him while pretending to play the role of her sister. Tucked inside her jacket pocket was the two thousand dollars Angela had promised him to keep tabs on her source, but she wouldn't give it to him, until he told her just who this person was.

She eyed her purse and then looked to make sure the pepper spray Jason had given her was still inside, and with a sigh, she dug her hands into her jacket pockets, burrowed deeper into its collar, and leaned back in the seat, settling in for a long wait. Her cell buzzed from the console of her car, and she didn't have to look down to see who it was. Ethan. It was his fifth call that morning. No doubt, his colleagues had told him what she'd done, and he was calling for an explanation. She reached down and sent his call to voicemail, just as she'd done to his last four calls.

* * *

Around seven thirty that evening, Sophie was beginning to have a newfound respect for cops on stakeouts, because she was ready to pull her hair out. How much longer? Didn't he have to go to the corner store or something? Sure, it was a weeknight, but he struck her as the type of young guy with an active social life. She banked on him wanting to go to a club to relax after getting out of jail or go visit some girl. Maybe he'd grabbed his things last night and found some other place to hold up for a while.

She was working up the nerve to see if the manager would be cooperative enough to give her his room number in exchange for fifty bucks when she saw someone fitting Josh's description come out to the front of the motel. She sat up and watched with delight as he hailed a cab. When they drove away, she merged her car into traffic behind them. It was a good thing she was familiar with San Francisco streets as the cab driver apparently was. With all the twists and turns he had been doing and weaving in and out of traffic, a less experienced driver would have lost them. For a moment, she panicked at the thought that Carelli had guessed he was being followed, but eventually the cab came to a stop in front of a club in the seedier section of downtown. Sophie drove past them and then made a quick U-turn. She then pulled into the first available parking spot and shut off her car. From her vantage point, she watched as Carelli paid the cab driver and waited just outside the club. It was Wednesday, so only a handful of people milled about outside.

She hoped he would go inside. She wasn't exactly dressed for the club, and it had been ages since she'd been inside one, but she would feel more comfortable approaching him in a public place with plenty of witnesses. But he didn't seem to be interested in going inside the club, or anywhere for that matter. He leaned against the brick wall, searching up and down the street and looking all too cocky and sure of himself. Clearly, he was waiting for someone.

As soon as she had the thought, Sophie saw a dark car appear almost immediately. Carelli dropped his stance, walked over to the car, and leaned down. A brief exchange took place and then he stepped away, just as the car pulled away. Sophie ducked lower in her seat as the car moved past her. She lifted her head slightly, but could only make out a partial license plate as it sped down the street. She turned back to Josh and watched as he brought his pinky to his nose and sniffed.

A little voice inside her told her she was in way over her head. Maybe she should call Ethan and tell him where she was. He had more experience in questioning suspects. He could get the answers she needed. But then she'd also have to explain why she refused to press charges and then she would have to tell him what Carelli said to her, and she wasn't entirely sure if she could trust him with that information yet. Deciding quickly, she grabbed for her purse, took the pepper spray out, and stuffed it into her other jacket pocket. Then she got out of the car and walked toward Carelli with her hands tucked into her pockets, clutching the money in one hand and the pepper spray in the other.

He didn't notice her until she was nearly upon him. When he did look up, he stepped back and looked around in fear. When he saw she was alone, his eyes narrowed on her in anger.

"Where's your asshole boyfriend?"

"I'm alone," she said, still not removing her hands from her pockets.

"That fucker broke my nose."

He didn't need to tell her. The white bandage on his nose, and the ugly black and blue bruises around it said it all.

"I'm sorry about that. But to be fair, he did think you were attacking me."

"Yeah, whatever. Did you follow me here to give me what you promised me?" he asked, changing the subject.

She lifted one hand out of her jacket pocket and patted it. "Two thousand as promised, but I need some information from you first."

She paused as a crowd of laughing women walked by them and into the club, and then she stepped closer to him.

"You said you turned off the video when my source entered the hotel, but I think they may have something to do with that murder," I said, making this up on the fly.

"I told you I want nothing to do with that."

"I'm not going to involve you."

Now came the tricky part. How the hell did she get this guy to tell her who the source was when she was supposed to already know the source?

"Just be careful. This person is helping me write a big story, but I'm not sure I can trust them."

"That's funny, because they just said the same thing about you."

Sophie froze. "What?"

"They said you're that dead bitch's sister. Showed me a picture and everything. You're her twin, and she was the one who I made the deal with."

She inhaled a breath and let it out slowly. "Okay. I'm sorry for deceiving you. That was my sister, and I'm trying to find out who killed her."

"Enough talk, lady. Give me my money."

"Who said I couldn't be trusted?"

"Your sister's snitch. Who else? They just drove off," he said, angling his head in the direction of the car that pulled away from the curb only moments ago.

Goddammit! She looked down the street and saw nothing but traffic lights.

"Who was it? What did they look like?" she asked, hearing the desperation in her voice.

He looked at her as if she'd grown two heads. "Bitch, are you crazy or something? Just give me the damn money!"

"Not until you tell me who that was."

Fast as lightning, he pulled something from his back jeans pocket, and before she could blink, he was aiming a gun at her forehead.

"This place isn't exactly deserted." She spoke calmly but trembled on the inside.

"By the time anybody notices, you'll be dead and twitching on the ground, and I'll be long gone. All for what? Two thousand dollars?" He held out his free hand. "Give it up. Now."

He was right. She'd be no help to Angela if she wound up dead, too. Besides, her mind was already spinning with the possibility that maybe the club had cameras, and she could get a look at the driver of the car.

She pulled the envelope from her jacket pocket and went to hand it to him.

"Just tell me if it was a man or a woman," she said in one last ditch effort to get something out of him.

But just as he reached for the envelope of money, she noticed his hands were shaking. She looked up into his eyes just in time to see them roll to the back of his head. The gun dropped from his hand, and he fell to the ground.

She tucked the money back into her pocket and knelt over him. "Are you all right? What's wrong?"

White foam flooded his mouth.

"Help," she screamed, looking around. "Help!"

For a street that seemed to have been deserted only moments before, several people were now beginning to crowd around the two of them.

"Call 9-1-1," she heard somebody yell.

"He's seizing," another cried out.

She looked back down at Josh and covered her mouth in shock and horror at the sight of him jerking and convulsing uncontrollably with saliva coming from his mouth. His eyes were opened in terror and his nose was bleeding profusely.

Sophie stood slowly and hadn't realized she was backing away in fear until someone grabbed her from behind. One arm locked securely about her waist and turned her around.

"Ethan," she cried with a mix of both panic and utter relief.

He didn't say anything but bore into her with cold, hard eyes. Then he pulled out his cell phone.

"This is Sergeant Ethan Markham requesting EMTs at..."

Sophie listened as he rattled off the address, Carelli's identity, and symptoms.

"Possible narcotic overdose or narcotic poisoning."

When he ended the call, he pulled her away from the crowd.

"Come with me," he gritted between clenched teeth.

When they got back to her car, he wrenched open the

door, practically tossed her into the driver's seat, and then slammed the car door and leaned down to glare at her through the open window.

"Are you okay to drive?"

"What?"

She thought he was going to yell at her, but his voice was surprisingly soft, despite the rage building in his eyes.

"Can you drive?"

"Yes, I'm fine. Maybe I should—"

"What you should do is go home immediately, stay there and wait for me."

"Ethan—"

"Go home now, Sophie!"

She looked into his eyes and the fierceness they held warned her to not argue with him any further. She nodded, turned the ignition, and sped away just as the sound of sirens pierced the night.

CHAPTER NINETEEN

ailey hated that she was being called out to a scene when she wasn't even on call. She especially despised the fact that the scene she was called to involved one of her colleagues. A colleague who was supposed to be keeping his hands clean until this case is solved.

She stood just outside the club's entrance, watching forensics thoroughly detail everything. She then spotted Ethan, walked up to him, and the two of them stood together in silence for nearly a minute before he spoke.

"Go ahead, say it."

She smiled sadly. "I'm experiencing some déjà vu. This is the second time this month I've been called to a scene where there's a dead body, and you are only yards away."

"Lucky me."

"What were you doing here, Ethan?"

"I wanted to know why Carelli attacked Sophie, so I got his last known address from his arrest record. It was some flea bag motel in the Tenderloin. He wasn't there, but he got to know some of the other guests, and they told me he liked to frequent this club a lot. When I got here, I saw the crowd, ran up, and saw him appearing to go through a seizure. I called EMTs and waited."

"Word for word from your statement," she said.

He shrugged.

Hailey eyed him balefully. "You sure that's how you want to play it?"

"Play what? That's my statement. Take it or leave it."

"I'm going to leave it, because it's fifty percent bullshit, and you and I both know it!"

She didn't mean to lose her temper with him so quickly, but it hurt a little to know he was starting to think twice about confiding in his fellow cops—confiding in her.

She sighed heavily. He obviously wanted to do this the hard way. "You know the club owner was gracious enough to give the uniforms access to the cameras. There's video of a black sedan approaching Carelli just before his death. It was too dark to see the driver."

"Tough break."

"Yes, it is, but after the car pulls away, guess who the camera spots him talking to?" Hailey didn't wait for him to answer but continued. "And only moments after he starts convulsing, guess who I see pull her away from the crowd?"

Ethan only returned her stare, and Hailey stepped up to him and hoped he took the steely gaze of her blue eyes seriously.

"Give me a reason why I shouldn't haul your ass in right now?"

"The car who drove up to him didn't belong to her."

"Says you. We didn't get a clear view of the license plate. You two are becoming quite a pair, Ethan." She cocked her head to one side and narrowed her eyes. "Did this closeness begin before or after your partner's murder?"

"Watch it, Hailey. She just wants to find her sister's killer."

She stepped back, forced herself to take a few calming breaths, and then tried for a more tactful approach. "Look, I believe you. I'm probably the only person who does, but I'm not going to be so trusting when it comes to her."

"She's stuck in the middle of this just like I am. She was attacked by Carelli, remember?"

"Whom she later refused to press charges against," Noah said, joining the conversation. "So instead of pressing charges against the man who may have had material evidence in her sister's death, she decides to follow him, and hours later, he's dead from a cocaine poisoning."

Ethan was now staring out at the street traffic slowing to a crawl as onlookers tried to get a glimpse of what happened from all the blue and red lights flashing.

"I'll call you," he said and headed to his car.

"Leave her alone, Ethan," she called after him, knowing he wouldn't heed her advice.

CHAPTER TWENTY

*T*wo months earlier...
"Hello?"

"Ethan, hi. It's me, Angie."

"Hi. Are you here in the city?"

"No, I'm in L.A."

Pause.

"What's wrong?" Angie asked.

"Nothing. It's just that you sound so much like Sophie."

"Yeah, we got that a lot growing up. Oh, speaking of Sophie, I talked to her, and she told me the same thing I told you. She just needs time, Ethan. She thought she was finally getting past everything with that trial, and then when Jason died, it brought everything back up again."

"I get it."

"But you don't like it."

He chuckled but changed the subject. "What can I do for you?"

"I meant what I said when we last spoke. You used to be able to talk to me about anything. I hope that hasn't changed because I'm a journalist. I wouldn't betray your confidence."

"I know."

"When we had dinner the other night, you looked like you had a lot on your mind. And I can even still hear it in your voice. Is it about the trial? Jason? Sophie?"

"All of the above."

"Well, let's take one topic and start from there. The trial, and just so you can feel comfortable, I'll say it: This entire conversation is off the record."

He chuckled again. "Fair enough. Okay, Angie. You win."

"Good, but I have one condition."

"I was wondering when you'd get to the catch."

She laughed. "It's nothing like that. I only ask that when you want to talk to me, you call this number. Don't come by the office or my apartment."

He frowned. "Is something wrong?"

"It's just a way to keep your privacy. If we're seen meeting too frequently, it could get around that your giving me information on the SFPD."

He nodded his head, but then realized she couldn't see him. "I hadn't thought of that. All right, we'll do it your way. But we are still friends, and when you get back into town, I'd like to take you to my favorite Italian spot in North Beach,"

He could sense her hesitancy, but he persisted. "Please, Angie. It's only dinner, and I promise not to break the 'meeting in person' rule again."

She sighed. "Okay. Just this once. I'll call you soon."

***

Sophie didn't remember how she'd gotten home, but she must have driven herself, because the next thing she knew, she was turning the key into the lock of her house. Once inside, she dropped her purse to the floor and then trudged to Jason's chair, sat down and stared at the opposite wall in a daze.

Josh Carelli was dead. What the hell was she going to do now? He had been her only lead, and now he was gone. Who else was going to tell her what was going on?

Her jacket was on, but she still felt a chill run through her body when she fixed on the sight of the young man on the ground twitching and convulsing violently. Her hands began to shake, so she clenched and unclenched them and then gave up altogether and covered her face with them.

She should call someone. She didn't want to be alone tonight, and she didn't have to be. Maybe, she could call… Who? Running through the mental list of people in her contacts list, she came to the sad conclusion that she spent way too much time alone.

Girlfriends were good for needing someone to just sit with her and distract her from thoughts of a man dying, but she didn't have many, aside from a few associates at the office. Angela was the one who made friends easily. Her sense of humor and natural ability to be the life of the party enticed people to be around her, and because Sophie was her twin sister, people just accepted her. Sophie often joked that if Angela weren't around, she wouldn't have any friends. Ironically, a week or so after her death, those who claimed to be Sophie's friends gradually drifted away. Without Angela serving as a liaison, they realized they didn't really have much in common with her. She wasn't funny, sociable, or the life of the party—not like Angela at all. She was just Sophie.

Ethan.

The name came to her so quickly, and just as quickly, she tossed it away. He'd said he was coming by to see her, but she didn't think he really would. He didn't want to see her. She'd lied to him, obstructed justice. Hell, even if he did answer the phone, she was not about to ask him to come sit with her, just because she was suddenly afraid of the dark.

She got up and went to her bag where she kept her cell in

the side pocket. She returned to the armchair, opened up her contacts list, and scrolled to the Ds. There were only two entries, one of them being a law clerk who worked with her named Diane Heller. She highlighted the other entry and hovered her thumb over the *send* key. She thought about the conversation she'd had with her dad about Jason. He wanted her to come to him, and now was her opportunity. After several seconds, she changed her mind and scrolled to the As. Angela's name was the only one listed. She dialed it and listened to five rings before her voicemail picked up.

"Hi, it's Angie James. I'm not available, but leave me a message and I'll return your call as soon as I can."

At the sound of her sister's voice, the same alto sound as her own, Sophie pressed the *end* button on her phone, lay to the side of the chair, and wept. After some time, her sobs had quieted, but she remained cuddled in the chair with her knees drawn up to her chest. That was the position she'd been sitting in when her doorbell sounded.

CHAPTER TWENTY-ONE

*W*hen Ethan pulled up to her house, he stared into the softly lit window of her living room for ten minutes.

He shouldn't be here. He hadn't liked what Hailey had implied, but the cop in him was on alert. What he hadn't told Hailey was that he knew without a doubt Sophie was hiding something—something key that could shed some light on this entire investigation. What he really wanted to do was haul her ass into an interrogation room and get the truth out of her the way he knew how to do. But Sophie James wasn't his usual suspect. She knew how cops worked. Not only was she smart, but that legal background of hers gave her an edge. She knew what questions were asked to get at the truth and the ones designed to incriminate.

He kept his eyes on the window, but there didn't seem to be any movement going on, so he figured she must be in her bedroom.

Screw it. He pulled the keys from the ignition, stepped out of the car, and slammed the door behind him. He had to go with his instincts and get whatever it was he needed out of her. If he really wanted his life back, she was a good place to start.

He rang her doorbell several times with no answer. Then he began knocking and started to grow a bit worried when there was still no answer.

"Sophie," he called through the door.

It may have been due to seeing Josh dead from an overdose, but Ethan could feel his panic level begin to rise. As a last resort, he looked down at his key ring and saw the spare key Jason had given him when they were partners. They'd exchanged keys in case of an emergency and one of them had to get entrance into the other's place.

He inserted the key into the lock and slowly pushed the door open, while grabbing for the gun he kept at the small of his back.

"Sophie? It's Ethan. Are you all right?"

Inside, he immediately noticed her purse on the floor by the door. The living room and kitchen were quiet. He headed upstairs and could hear the shower running before he reached the top. Relief swept through him, now knowing that this was the reason she didn't answer the door. Still, the whole atmosphere made him feel wary. As he slowly climbed the steps, he held his gun pointed down and against his thigh.

At the top of the stairs, he made his way toward her bedroom. It was also empty, but he kept moving toward the adjoining bathroom, where the shower continued to run, and the door was left ajar. He didn't want to scare her, but he also didn't like the idea of standing out there if something was wrong. If she was really taking a shower, he was going to feel like an asshole, but he wanted to see for himself she was okay.

Like Hailey, he was experiencing déjà vu. Only a couple of weeks ago, he'd entered a bathroom to find Angela dead, and God help him if he found Sophie like that.

"Sophie," he said softly and slowly pushed the door open.

His first view was of the counter where the sink and vanity rested. His eyes moved to the left, past the toilet, and finally rested on the glass shower. There, he saw her through the doors and froze.

She was sitting on the shower floor, her clothes from that night still on, but completely drenched now from the water spraying down on her. Her back was against the wall, her knees drawn up close to her chest with her arms wrapped tightly around them. Her chin was resting on her knees, and she looked to be staring straight ahead, focused on something only she could see. Ethan came into the bathroom, put his gun down next to the sink and edged slowly toward the shower.

"Sophie?"

She continued to stare straight ahead, although he could tell she knew he was there by the way her body shifted slightly at the sound of his voice. He opened the glass doors, knelt down and touched her arm, feeling the warm water spray his hand.

Very slowly, she turned her head to look at his hand and then up at him. Her eyes were clear as they seemed to study him.

"You shouldn't be here," she said.

He didn't respond to that, but rose to his feet and twisted the knob to turn the shower off. Then he turned and left the bathroom in search of a towel. He found a supply in a hall closet and returned to find her now standing in the shower. She'd removed her shirt and jeans and was down to nothing but her panties and bra with her wet hair clinging to her face. Ethan forced himself not to stare too long at her full breasts, slender waist, curved hips and thick thighs, but came toward her with the towel. As he wrapped her in it, he could feel her looking at him.

"Don't you think I know what your colleagues are saying about me?" she asked. "I'm not to be trusted."

With the towel wrapped tightly about her torso, he inched back toward the sink, determined to not touch her anymore.

"Look, Sophie, if you want to talk, I'm here."

She shook her head, stepped out of the shower, and came closer to him. Leaning forward, she braced her hands on the sink, trapping him between them. The way she looked at him with those wide, penetrating eyes, as though he were the only man in the world that mattered, made him go completely still.

"What are you doing?" he asked, not recognizing the sound of his own voice.

"Giving you what you came for."

"I didn't come for this."

"Didn't you?"

"No." It was the truth, but his body didn't agree.

"No need in playing coy, Ethan," she said and began kissing both sides of his neck, slowly and sensuously. Her lips were warm and wet, and he imagined that's how the rest of her body would feel.

"One tug and my towel comes right off," she said.

At the mention of her towel, he stared down at the spot that tucked the two ends together, where he saw the beginning curve of her breasts.

She was moving against him now, and he silently prayed for strength.

"I remember that summer. We couldn't get enough of each other."

"That's enough." He said it quietly but could feel irritation beginning to rise, despite how damn good she felt moving her hips against his crotch.

"Or were you disappointed it was me and not Angie?"

"Stop it, Sophie."

Her small hands gripped his forearms as she leaned back and looked at him with eyes pleading. "Why didn't you confide in me as much as you confided in her? You told her everything, but I was your girlfriend. Did you choose the wrong girl?"

"This isn't the time to talk about this."

She shrugged and leaned forward again. "Then touch me."

When he didn't move, she bit his earlobe and whispered, "What's the matter? Jason can't stop us anymore."

He shoved her away, furious with himself for caring too much to come here, furious that he still wanted her.

"What were you doing following Josh Carelli?"

He'd embarrassed her, but she recovered quickly. "Because he knew something about Angie's death."

"And you were going to question him? You're not a cop, Sophie."

"The cops are the ones who probably killed my sister!"

Ethan stared. "Is that what you really think?"

"She was about to expose that someone or a group of someones in the SFPD covered up Jason's death. That someone or someones got to her before she could. Josh was there that night at the hotel. I saw him at the desk when I went up to see Angie. He looked at me so strangely, but I didn't think anything about it at the time. Now, I believe he thought I was her."

She stalked past him out of the bathroom and into her bedroom. Ethan didn't follow after her, knowing she was probably changing out of that towel.

"You didn't press charges, because you wanted to talk to him alone?"

"I wanted him away from the SFPD. I thought he might feel safer opening up to me if there were no cops around."

When he finally came out of the bathroom, he saw she was wearing a fluffy white bathrobe.

"Why didn't you come to me?"

She had her arms braced over her dresser and was staring into the mirror directly at him. When their gazes locked, he already had his answer.

"You think I'm part of that cover up."

"Why were you following me?"

"Because you were attacked last night."

"Bullshit!" She whipped around and glared at him. "You're afraid, aren't you? You're afraid of what I know. You, Hailey, Noah, and everyone else in that homicide division think I know more than I'm telling. Well, let me tell you something, *Sergeant*: If I could prove that any of you bastards killed my sister or Jason, you wouldn't have to wonder. You'd all be locked up by now!"

He was across the room in two strides and had her arms locked in his grasp. "Do you think I killed Jason?"

She continued to glare at him.

"Answer me, Goddammit!" Then he lowered his voice and stared, trying to see the truth of what she thought of him. "Do you think I killed Jason?"

The first sign of tears welled in her eyes. "No," she said, on a whisper. "I just think you wanted to."

He realized he was still grasping her arms and immediately let her go and stepped back. He didn't know what to say to that. He never really admitted to himself how he felt about the night he found out his partner had been killed. But in quiet times, when he was all alone and allowed himself to think even one minute about it...

He didn't look at Sophie but started to brush past her and out of the bedroom, before she grabbed ahold of him.

"Ethan, wait."

"What?" he asked, sharply. He was ready to get the hell

out of there, away from her and away from memories of Jason.

"I'm sorry. I shouldn't have said that."

"Forget it."

"What happened in the bathroom. Thank you for not…"

"For not taking advantage of you? For not being the prick you think I am?"

She sighed. "I don't think that about you, Ethan. I never did."

He remained still, silently pleading with her to let him go before he really did take advantage of her.

"I wanted to say yes," she said. "That day when I was preparing you for trial and you asked me out? I should have said yes. In my heart, I knew Jason had checked out of our marriage. I couldn't prove it, but I just knew it. When you asked me out—"

"No," Ethan interrupted, vividly remembering that day when he'd caused her to become flustered. He remembered wanting to kiss her. "Then we would have been no better than him or Vanessa."

He forced one foot in front of the other and went down the stairs. He heard her soft footsteps trailing close behind, but he continued on until he was at the front door. There, he paused and turned to face her.

"I didn't kill Angela. I didn't kill Jason, either. But you were right. When I found out he was dead, all I could think about was what he put you through, and all the fucking humiliation for you, for me and my department. I felt relief. I never got to mourn him, because I kept feeling relief, and that scares me."

She stepped forward, wrapped her arms around his neck and hugged him tightly. "It's okay. I understand. I understand, Ethan."

She kept saying it over and over again as he wrapped his

arms tightly around her waist, buried his head at the crook of her neck, and allowed himself to be held. He didn't know how long they stood there holding each other in her doorway, but it felt so good, the comfort she was giving him felt so good, he didn't want it to end.

Then he felt a soft kiss on his cheek. And another. And another.

He lifted his head to look at her, and they stared at each other.

"Ethan," she said.

That soft utterance of his name was the final push he needed to break down the wall between them. He leaned down and kissed her with all the pent-up desire he'd been feeling for too damn long. He could feel her hesitation, but he didn't want to stop tasting her and kept going until she finally relented. She returned his kiss with a soft moan. Ethan wasted no time, and without relinquishing her lips, picked her up by the waist and carried her up the stairs. Once they were inside her bedroom, he kicked the door shut behind him and turned until her back was against the door. Lowering her to the ground, he attacked the button and zipper of his jeans. She untied her robe with one swift motion and bared herself to him.

At the sight of her breasts, he wished they could go slow, giving him the time to knead, kiss, and suckle them to his delight—to her delight. But they were moving so fast, and he felt like he was going to explode if he couldn't get inside her now.

He finally got his zipper down and was shoving his jeans off as she undid the knot in her hair. Black tresses fell to her face, and she looked so good standing there in a white robe against her beautifully toned skin with her hair tousled, it nearly brought him to his knees. Keeping his eyes on her, he stepped forward, grabbed her by the waist and put one hand between her legs.

"Ethan!"

She was wet and pliant, just as he'd been waiting for. Without another moment's thought, he lifted her once again and pushed himself inside her right there against the bedroom door.

Sophie's legs wrapped around him, as though it were the most natural movement in the world, and he drove into her again and again, whispering in her ear how goddamned good she felt. She clung to him, gripped the back of his head, taking his thrusts and chanting his name like a mantra. She bit into the meat of his shoulder and told him over and over again that she was coming. The thought excited him, drove him wild, and he increased his thrusting until her moans had grown louder and he could feel her tightening around him.

"That's it," he rasped in her ear. "Let me have it all."

She did, and he rode the wave of her orgasm until he felt his own climax overpower him. He tightened his grip on her waist, refusing to let her go, until at last, he was spent.

Very slowly, he lowered her to the floor. Unable to move, he leaned his forehead against her, still keeping his hands on her waist. They stayed like that for several moments, both struggling to catch their breaths.

"We're going to regret this in the morning," she said, looking up at him.

"Probably," he said, meeting her gaze. "But morning will be here soon enough. Right now, I want to try this in bed."

With that, he turned her toward the bed, lay her down, and promised himself that this time, he'd go slowly.

* * *

Ethan was lost in thought as he lay behind Sophie. He'd pulled the sheets down, slowly uncovering her torso, and lost himself in her body. He tried to ingrain in his memory every curve and dimple to be recalled later. He looked down toward her lower back and eyed the faded scar that was still evident to his touch, and then he wondered if this was the same scar from that night.

"What are you thinking about?"

He raised his eyes to meet hers as she turned her head to look up at him. He put one arm around her waist and pulled her closer to his chest. Then he asked her what had always been in the back of his mind.

"What did you see in Jason?"

She frowned. "Really, Ethan? Is that what you want to talk about now? Right here?"

"I've always wondered."

She pulled from his embrace, lay down onto the pillow, and sighed heavily. "I fell for Jason because he was so charming and dedicated to his work. He had such big plans. When he made Sergeant, he gave himself five years to become chief of police. I loved that, because my eye was on the position of San Francisco's DA. Our ambitions complemented each other, motivated each other. We would be the husband and wife team that put the bad guys away together."

She laughed with derision. "I don't know why I thought ambition alone would make a good marriage. Maybe a marriage of convenience, but that wasn't what I wanted. Maybe it was what he wanted."

Ethan didn't say anything, not wanting to interrupt her. He remembered the goals Jason used to set for himself, and he admired and respected him for it. Over a beer after work, Ethan could quote him many times saying: "I'm going to be your boss, someday, Markham." That might have been true if they hadn't landed the Johnson case.

"As the years went by, I finally admitted a truth about Jason that I ignored," Sophie said. "He was a playboy. He couldn't be faithful, but still loved the idea of being married. He wanted a power wife by his side. Someone he could feel proud of to put in front of the cameras with him. But when the cameras turned off, he could just be Jason and forget that he was married.

"With me still focused on my career, I ignored his transgressions and let the marriage waste away. I think eventually I would have grown tired of it, but I had no choice when Vanessa Johnson took the stand and confessed to her affair with him. Suddenly, the whole city knew everything about our private life and women whom I never met were looking at me, wondering what the hell I was going to do. To give Jason some credit, I think he realized the dilemma I was in. He moved out without me having to ask him to, and I felt so relieved."

One solitary tear traced down her cheek, but she made no move to wipe it away. "Then when he was murdered, I felt so guilty."

Ethan brushed the lone tear away with his thumb. "I shouldn't have come by that night. I heard he moved out, but I didn't come there to take advantage of you, Sophie. I wanted to make sure you were all right. I didn't think he would show up, but that's no excuse. I should have just stayed away."

"Sophie," Jason called as he entered the house.

"I'm in the kitchen," she said, while still looking at Ethan. Her eyes seemed to be telling him to just keep quiet.

"I came back to get a few more of my things. I just need—" He stopped when he came into the kitchen and saw Ethan standing there.

"What are you doing here?" Jason asked, sounding instantly on guard.

Ethan looked him directly in the eye and told him the truth. "I came to check up on Sophie. These last few weeks have been hell on all of us."

"Sophie?" Jason emphasized her name. "You're calling her by her nickname and you're dropping by while I'm not at home. Looks like you two have gotten more comfortable without me."

Then he looked down at the floor to the spilled tea and broken cups. "What the hell happened in here?"

"I was about to clean it up," Sophie explained. "Just get what you need and leave."

Jason looked to Sophie and gave her a look mixed with anger, hurt, and Ethan guessed, betrayal. Suddenly, he must have realized he didn't have the right to feel any of those emotions and chuckled with scorn.

"You know what, partner? I can't decide what Sophie is more angry about. Is it the fact that I was unfaithful or the fact that I caused her to lose that cushy new job at Becker and Reynolds?"

"Get out," Sophie said, an edge of finality in her tone. "Get your things later."

"Whatever you say, honey."

He left the kitchen and Sophie went after him to make sure, Ethan supposed, that he was leaving. Jason grabbed his jacket and shoved it on in angry, jerking movements. He stomped to the door, threw it open, and turned back to glare at them both.

"You have my permission to fuck my wife, friend."

"You're disgusting," Sophie said, tears coming to her eyes.

Jason barely spared her a glance but looked back to Ethan, the anger in his eyes for the moment gone, replaced by open truth and despair.

"I've seen the way he looks at you."

Coming back to the present, Ethan stared at a spot in the ceiling, remembering those words from his partner. Then he looked down and saw that Sophie was staring up at him as though she were recalling the same memory.

"After he left, I waited around long enough to see that you were okay," Ethan said. "But I was ashamed to look at you, not only because of the trial, but because Jason had seen through me, and I was sure you'd seen it too. He was right, you know. I did want you. I always did."

"You don't have to say anything."

"For all my attempts to treat you as my partner's wife, and the ADA, to remain professional even almost cold toward you, he could see right through it."

Sophie sat up, wrapping the sheet around her breasts. Ethan watched her smooth bare back reminded him of milk chocolate, and he ached to run his hands over her. He sat up behind her and breathed out.

"I didn't kill him."

She whipped her head around to face him. "I know that."

"Do you?"

She stood and made a dash for the bathroom. But before she could shut herself behind the door, Ethan was right behind her, took her by the arm and turned her around to face him.

"I know you were helping Angela find Jason's killer. I knew you were just waiting for her to give you a name so you could prosecute. Would you have still prosecuted if she gave you my name?"

"Please let me go," she said, softly.

"I went to see him that night he died. I wanted to talk to him."

"Ethan, stop." She struggled against him, but he gripped her arm and led her back to the bed to sit her down.

"It's time we talked about that night he died. I mean really talk."

"Why? What difference does it make now?"

"Because you were his wife, and because I'm tired of looking at you and seeing doubt in your eyes about me."

She looked at him, and he could see the denial forming on her lips, but then she stopped and that was enough confirmation for him.

"Sophie—"

"I told you I don't want to talk about this."

"Sophie, wait. One more question. Look at me." He waited until she turned around. "Did you ever tell him about us?"

"There was no need to. It was a kiss, and we stopped ourselves."

"I meant Fourth of July. That summer."

She was quiet for so long, and he knew she was reliving long ago memories.

"No," she said. "I never told him."

"We've had a hard time trying to reach you, Ms. Sykes," Hailey said, placing a bottle of water in front of the tall and attractive middle-aged woman.

Anita took the water with a grateful nod, twisted off the cap, and took a sip before slowly putting it down. She looked up at Hailey and Noah from her seat in Hailey's office.

"I'm sorry. My daughter just had her first baby, and I flew up to Portland to stay with her and help get her and the baby settled."

Noah frowned. "Is the cell service bad in Portland? You could have returned our numerous calls."

"Yes, I could have." She paused, took another sip of water and seemed to be trying to steady her breathing. "But I was waiting."

Hailey leaned forward in her seat from across the cluttered desk. "Waiting? Waiting for what?"

"You can call it a directive. I didn't know what to do. When I got back to work, one of the girls who work the front desk told me what happened. If I had known, I would have never..." She trailed off and looked at the two of them with pleading eyes. "I wasn't deliberately trying to get rid of evidence."

Noah, who had been standing over Anita the entire time she was talking, must have sensed her distress. He came around the desk and sat in the other visitor's chair beside her. Hailey watched as he put a comforting hand on her shoulder and proceeded to soften his tone.

"Ms. Sykes, take a few deep breaths and start from the beginning."

She did what he said, and when Hailey felt she was calm, she began asking questions.

"Tell us exactly what happened that night before you left for the airport."

"I was on my way out and the phone rang."

"What time was this?"

"It was a few minutes after seven. I know because I looked at the time on my phone. I almost didn't answer, because I was in such a rush, but I did, and I did this one favor. I knew something wasn't right, but I felt it was the only way to pay back a debt."

"What was the favor?"

"The digital video footage for the last two hours."

"And you just handed that over?"

"Yes, but you don't understand," she said, her voice rising in panic. "I owed him so much for helping my family when we lost our niece a few years back. He used to work in your Missing Persons department, and without his help, I don't think we would have ever found her. I just wanted to make things right and do something for him in return."

Hailey's blood went cold. She didn't even have to ask, but she needed to hear the name for the record. She leaned even farther in her seat toward Anita. "Ms. Sykes, who called you? Who asked for that digital footage?"

CHAPTER TWENTY-THREE

Ethan woke the next morning to the sunlight seeping through the closed blinds, and for the first time in weeks, he felt the surprising urge to get up, open them, and let light fill the room. Then he rolled over to his other side, saw the pillow and empty space beside him, and the memories of last night began to flood his mind.

He could appease his conscience by telling himself his intentions had been good from the beginning—that he hadn't come there with the purpose of sleeping with her, but it wouldn't help. No matter how many ways he tried to excuse himself, he was still lying naked in Sophie's bed—in a bed she once shared with Jason.

He could almost recall the exact moment he'd decided to chuck his morals out the window last night. When she told him she'd regretted not accepting his offer for a Friday night date, those words had done his ego wonders. And as they stood there at her front door holding each other, he couldn't forget how good she'd smelled, and how soft and inviting she'd felt. He'd wanted nothing more than to lose himself in her, just like he had when he was in his twenties.

Ethan groaned as he felt himself grow hard again with the memory of that second time, which had been slower, more practiced, and felt even better than the first. He'd been able to explore all of her, gradually bringing her to climax and back down. After his own release, he silently admitted defeat and brought her close to him, where they both slept and waited for the morning's regret. But there was no regret.

He rose from the bed, grabbed his t-shirt and jeans, which were still in a crumpled heap by the door, and pulled them on. He then left the bedroom and made his way downstairs, following the scent of coffee.

She was sitting at a small table in her kitchen area, dressed casually in a UC BerkeleyT-shirt and gray sweatpants, studying some papers in front of her. He noticed a cardboard box at her feet, and every now and then, she'd reach inside the box and pull out some more manila folders and papers.

She looked up when she heard him. Her hair was brushed back into a ponytail and God help him, she looked even more desirable in the light of day. He smiled, hoping to ease any lingering tension, but instead of returning the gesture, she angled her head toward the stove.

"There's breakfast on the skillet if you're hungry."

He shook his head. "Just tell me you have coffee."

She nodded to the coffeepot resting on the countertop. "Mugs are in the cabinet above, sugar is on the counter. Milk and cream are in the fridge."

He frowned. Her answers sounded clipped and much too professional for a woman who'd spent the better part of the night telling him how good he felt inside her. But he let her mannerisms go for the moment and poured himself the coffee. Leaving out the cream and sugar, he carried the mug to the table and sat down across from her.

"What's all this?" he asked.

She pushed a stack of manila folders toward him. "Last night, before you came by, I got a visit from one of Angie's colleagues. She told me she and Angie had been sharing storage space for over a year. When she heard about her death, she didn't know what to do with this box of stuff."

"Why didn't she turn it over to the police?" Ethan asked, opening one of the folders.

Sophie shrugged her reply. "She said she skimmed through everything and saw mostly articles and copies of interviews Angie wrote years ago. She didn't think they'd be any use to the police."

He looked up as Sophie gave him a sly smile. "Lucky for us."

"Why is that?" he asked.

"Because she didn't look closely enough." Sophie motioned to the folder he was still reading through. "Keep going and you'll find profiles on every cop working in the homicide division along with their connection, if any, to Jason."

Ethan looked up. "She was establishing motives."

She nodded. "And opportunity. Those with any remote connection to Jason have a location written by their name, stating where they'd been at the time of his death."

Ethan skimmed the list. "The Lieutenant's name is on here, too." He glared up at her. "He didn't kill Jason."

"I'm not saying he did or didn't, Ethan. I'm just showing you Angie's thought process."

He glanced at the list again and found his name:

Ethan Markham, Jason's partner for five years.

Location at the time of Jason's death:

That part was left blank. He read quickly through the rest of the list and found she'd established alibis for everyone at the time of Jason's death except for him. He looked up at Sophie and knew she'd noticed the same thing.

He set the papers aside and took a sip of his coffee. "Hand this over to Hailey and Noah the first chance you get. In fact, I'll take it with me when I leave and drop it off at the station."

"Ethan, there could be something in here that proves who killed Jason, and I'm betting you've come to the same conclusion that whoever killed Jason also killed Angie. She probably found out the truth, and now she's dead."

"Cross and Sayres are investigating her murder. Give this to them, and let them do their jobs."

"But I can help."

"You mean help like you did with Carelli? If you hadn't dropped the charges and let him stay in jail to be questioned, we might be closer to tracking down a murderer and not sending another body to the fucking morgue!"

She glared at him for what seemed like an eternity and then grabbed all the folders and papers and stacked them neatly in the box.

Ethan ducked his head, counted to ten, and then slowly raised it. He was tired of tiptoeing around the elephant in the room.

"Should we talk about last night?"

"For what? Last night was last night. It happened. End of story."

She didn't say anything more but continued rummaging through the box. Then she stopped. Ethan leaned forward, curious as to what snagged her attention, but before he could see it, she was already reaching her hand inside the box and pulling it out. She opened her palm and showed him, but when Ethan saw it, he didn't want to take it.

* * *

August 2002

"Are you all right?"

He had been staring off up at the ceiling, wondering to himself what the hell he was doing, when her sleepy voice broke into his thoughts. He looked down at the young woman, who was now curled against his chest and staring up at him with wide, questioning brown eyes.

He brought his arm down from underneath the pillow and wrapped it around her waist to bring her closer.

"I'm good."

"I was watching you for a few minutes. You were deep in thought," she said.

"I was just thinking about my application for the academy," he lied and leaned down to kiss her soft lips. "I haven't heard anything back yet."

"You'll get in," Sophie said, smiling. "Your mom must be so proud of you."

He nodded. "She says it all the time."

She opened her mouth to speak, closed it, and then opened it again. "What about your dad?"

He stiffened. "What about him?"

"Have you tried contacting him? I'm sure he would—"

To stop the question, he kissed her again. She returned the kiss and continued to stare up at him for a moment longer before pulling away and rising from the bed.

"Where are you going?"

She started pulling on her panties and bra and the dress she'd worn last night on their date. "I should get home. Angie told my dad I was staying at a friend's house. I'll see you later."

He sprang out of bed and hopped into his boxers. By the time he reached for her arm and gently pulled her around, she was almost out of his bedroom.

"Wait a minute. What just happened?"

She seemed to take a minute to calm herself and sighed.

"Nothing. I'm sorry. I had a good time last night. I should get home."

"I thought Angie was covering for you," he said, reaching for a strand of her hair.

She paused. "She is."

"Look, you don't have to leave now. Let's go have breakfast."

"I really can't."

"Okay, but hang on. There's something I want to give you."

He hadn't planned on doing this now, but he had it in his pocket, and suddenly he felt a burst of courage shoot through him. Without a second thought, he stalked toward the spot where she was sitting, knelt beside her, and tucked his hand beneath her chin, forcing her to look at him.

Before the surprise in her eyes could ward him off, he kissed her. It was a chaste kiss at first, and then he used his tongue to probe her mouth open. When her lips parted ever so slightly, he invaded her and the kiss deepened. God, she tasted so sweet. He moved his hands to the sides of her face and brought her closer. He loved her and wanted her near him always. He still couldn't understand how a dumb kid like him could fall so far, so dangerously hard, for a girl after only a month of dating her, but there it was. Maybe, he'd always been in love with her, long before he even knew what these feelings meant.

He reluctantly pulled away from her and saw she had a dazed look of surprise.

"Sorry about that," he muttered.

She pressed two fingers to her lips as Ethan pulled the small jewelry case from his pocket. When he opened it to reveal the bracelet winking at them, the surprise on her face turned blank and for a while, he couldn't tell what she was thinking.

"I think this should say it all," he began. "But if not...I want you to be my girl, Sophie. Wait for me."

There. It was out, and now all he could do was shut up and wait for her reply. But she only stared at it. She stared for so long he began to grow nervous. Then, she slowly began to reach for the bracelet and then instantly withdrew her hand as though its slightest touch would singe her fingers.

"I'm sorry," she said. "You have the wrong girl, Ethan."

* * *

He stared at her for a long time, wondering if she was remembering that day he gave it to her, and how she made him feel like an idiot for saving his money to buy it and eager to see the look on her face when he gave it to her.

"Thanks," he muttered, took the jewelry case from Sophie, and clutched it in his hand. He wouldn't tell her that as soon as he returned home, he was putting it in a desk drawer and forgetting it ever existed.

Her tone turned sour. "I see you didn't waste time."

He knew what she meant but refused to be baited by her. "It's not what you think."

"What am I thinking?"

"That I'd tried my luck with your sister, but you're wrong. You know I wouldn't do that. You said I had the wrong girl."

"You did. You asked me to be your girlfriend, but I'm not the one you confided in that summer."

He stepped forward. "Is this why we broke up? Is this what you believed about me? You think I was trying to satisfy some twin fantasy?"

Her chin rose defiantly. "Weren't you? You told her everything that was important to you. Do you know why I asked about your dad? Because you told Angie about him, and how he asked to come to your college graduation, but you told him you didn't want him there. Was that so hard to tell me?"

"No, it wasn't, but—"

"But I was just a good time for you that summer."

He reached her and took her by the arms, wanting to shake some sense into her. "Yes, I did tell her about my dad. I even told her I'd given you this bracelet and that you refused it. I was angry and hurt and wanted to toss it into bay, but she offered to hold onto it for me just in case you had a change of heart. But the summer ended, and apparently, so did you and me."

She shook herself free of him, and he could see she was fighting a battle within herself to believe him.

"When did you start believing the worst about me?"

"When you started lying to me."

"What did I lie to you about?"

She let go a heavy sigh. "I never told you her room number."

He frowned in confusion. "What?"

"Angie's hotel room. I never told you her room number. How did you know where to find me?"

A loud pounding sounded at Sophie's front door, and Ethan slowly released her as they both turned toward the noise, frowning. Sophie nearly went for the door, but Ethan stopped her, gave her a look, and went to investigate himself. When he peered through the peep hole, he paused and lowered his head, shaking it. *Damn.*

"Who is it?" Sophie asked on a whisper.

The pounding came again. Ethan backed away from the door and walked past her toward the living room where he kept his shoes and jacket.

"Ethan," she called.

"They're going to take me in. Let me get my shoes on."

"Wait—what? Who's taking you in? Who's at the door?"

"Cross and Sayres," he said. "Go ahead and let them in."

She ignored the pounding at the door and went after Ethan. "Tell me what's going on. What do they want with you?" She kneeled down in front of him as he sat on the edge of the sofa, lacing up his sneakers. "I'm still a lawyer, Ethan. I can advise you."

He snorted out a laugh. "You're not going to want to help me with this."

Another knock sounded, and this time they both heard Hailey through the closed front door. "Ms. James, it's the police. Open the door, please."

Sophie didn't move. "I'm not answering that door until you tell me what this is about."

He finished tying his sneakers and stared into her eyes. He was about to give her another reason to believe the worst about him.

"You were right. You didn't have to tell me the room number, because I already knew it. I was there at the hotel that night. I went to see Angela the night she was killed."

CHAPTER TWENTY-FOUR

hen Angela opened the door to her hotel room, he noticed she did it slowly and with caution. When she saw it was him, her eyes widened in surprise. There was another emotion, but she masked it so well he didn't have time to name it.

"Ethan," she said, saying his name as though she were testing the sound of it on her lips.

He took advantage of her surprise by pushing the door open wider, stepping inside the room, and shutting it behind him. "You don't ask who it is before you open the door?"

"I was expecting someone, but not you. Why are you here?"

"You haven't returned my calls in over a week, and you want to know why I'm here?"

She frowned. "I'm sorry. Work has been hectic, and I'm on deadline. Can I offer you something to drink?"

Without waiting for a reply, she went for the small refrigerator where water, soft drinks, and miniature bottles of alcohol were stored.

"Yeah, I heard about your deadline. Is this the same story you're supposedly writing about me? About Jason?"

"It is, and the person I'm expecting to see was going to help me finish it up."

"You mean help label me as a murderer."

She handed him the bottle of water, and another frown creased her brow. "What exactly do you think you know, Ethan?"

"I know for months you've been trying to get information out of me, knowing I'd fall back on our friendship and tell you everything, and now I hear you have a source who says I killed my partner."

It seemed as if her entire body stilled, and she was playing the confused role very well. He would have believed her if he didn't already know she was a liar.

"I'm not sure who's been feeding you information, but I'll admit I wasn't entirely truthful about why I moved here from L.A.," she said, glancing at her wristwatch. "I knew that after everything happened, Sophie was going to need comfort and emotional support, and our dad isn't the cuddliest of men. I always liked San Francisco, but what clinched the deal for me was Sophie and the chance to write an investigative story about Jason's murder."

"What's left to write about?" Ethan asked. "The case has gone cold."

She seemed to hesitate. "That's true, but my source tells me the reason the investigation stalled is because the homicide department —your department—covered it up."

He reacted instantly. "Your source is a goddamn liar. We spent weeks, months, tracking down every lead and snitch we could find who could give us Jason's killer. There's no way it was covered up."

"But the trial—"

"Fuck the trial."

"He embarrassed the department."

"He was still a cop!"

"I'm not going to argue with you. I have my information." He noticed as she slowly breathed in and out. "You don't get it do you? This isn't just about you. This story, this whole fucking mess is one year in the making."

"Who's your source?"

"You know I can't tell you that."

He shook his head and tried his best to get ahold of his temper. When he spoke again, he kept his tone calm and firm.

"I'm telling you this because I've always liked you, and your family was very good to me and my mom. Let this go. You're playing a dangerous game. You're going to regret going down this road."

"Are you threatening me?"

"That's a promise."

* * *

"Is that all?"

Ethan looked around the four walls of the interview room, feeling out of sorts that he was on the opposite side of an interrogation. He looked over at Noah who'd asked the question.

"That's it. After I said those words, I left. But on my way home, I thought about what she said, wondered about her being alone in that hotel room and then called Anita."

"For the digital tapes."

"That's right."

"Why?"

"Because I wanted to know who she was meeting. She kept looking at her watch. She tried to seem unbothered, but I could tell in her face she was nervous and wanted me to leave as soon as possible."

"Well, you got a good look at the footage." Noah's tone dripped with sarcasm. "Who was she meeting?"

"I don't know."

"Don't bullshit us, Markham."

Ethan didn't react but continued in a calm tone. "The

video cut off about thirty minutes after I left. I don't know who she met after me."

Noah now stood to his feet and leaned over the table toward him. "Then why keep it? You knew we were investigating this case and needed that video. You should've handed it over to us. You never should've taken it to begin with without a warrant!"

"I needed some time to work it out."

"You're not on this case."

Ethan didn't move a muscle but met Noah's glare with his own. "I wasn't going to be a suspect either."

"Too damn late."

Hailey, who had been quiet this whole time, put a hand over Noah's as a silent urging for him to calm down. All the while, she kept her eyes on Ethan.

"You see how this looks, don't you?" she asked. You left Angela's hotel room, then called your friend to give you digital footage of the hotel. Then Angela is murdered and instead of handing the footage over, you keep it and now claim the video cuts off after you leave her room."

She paused for a long time, and he assumed she was giving him time to process the seriousness of it all. He didn't know what she expected him to say, but he wasn't about to admit that it looked bad even though it did.

"You gave yourself motive and opportunity," she said.

"I didn't kill her."

"What about Sophie?"

This time he did react. "No."

"She was there, Ethan."

"She didn't kill her sister."

Silence fell between the three of them, until Hailey let go a deep sigh. "You're trying to tell me we're looking for a third mystery guest?"

"It would seem so."

Noah scoffed and then turned to his partner. Hailey moved her eyes from Ethan to Noah and very subtly shook her head. Noah glared at Ethan once more and then stood from his seat and left the interview room.

"Don't do me any favors, Hailey."

"Don't flatter yourself. The only reason I'm not arresting you is because I actually believe you. But I'm sorry to say IAD is going to want to talk to you again this afternoon. You're going to need to convince them again that you're not a murderer." She gathered her legal pad and also rose from her seat. "In the meantime, hand over that footage, and keep your ass as far away from my case as possible."

She headed for the door, opened it, and then stopped and turned toward him.

"There was no third guest. I know she had something to do with her sister's death and now Carelli's. I'm going to prove it, and you're going to stay the hell out of my way, or I'll be arresting you right along with her."

CHAPTER TWENTY-FIVE

Sophie had wanted to follow Ethan to the station and advise him on when to speak and when to claim his fifth amendment right, but he outright refused. Sophie didn't like it, but in the end, she backed down. Maybe it was best she wasn't in the interview room, sitting beside him while the inspectors asked him questions about being the last person to see Angela alive—just like Jason.

Jesus, was this really happening again?

At Ethan's insistence, she also gave up the box of papers to Hailey and Noah. It was true, she was no cop, and she'd already done enough interfering in the investigation. But that evidence did nothing but only shine a brighter spotlight on Ethan. According to Angela's notes, he didn't have an alibi for Jason's murder, and the fact that she was singling him out gave Ethan a motive to kill her, too.

Sophie recalled that day on the ferry with her sister, and it seemed as if Angela wanted to exonerate Ethan, despite what her source had claimed. Did she have a change of heart and eventually come to believe that the man they both knew as a teenager was actually a stranger?

She'd never told him the room number.

The thought first came to her at the funeral, but it was so fleeting, and she'd dismissed it immediately with the excuse that Ethan was a cop, and he could've flashed his badge at the front desk to get Angela's room number. But then she continued to remember when he left her office that same afternoon. He was so angry with her, and even more so, with Angela. It was likely he would try to track her down and force her to tell him the truth about the rumors circulating about him and a cover-up. She wondered to herself what they had talked about when he found her.

Sophie went for her cell phone, which she'd left in her purse on the kitchen counter, and scrolled through the text messages, until she came to the last one Angela sent her.

I know what you did. Why Sophie?

She put the phone down and could feel a dull ache slowly forming at the back of her head. If Angela knew, it was apparent she didn't tell Ethan, because he would have confronted her with the truth a long time ago. She rubbed the back of her neck and took several deep breaths. She couldn't do this anymore. She had to stop these racing thoughts. If she continued to stand here and speculate about Ethan, Angela, and the night she'd died, it would only lead her to thoughts of Ethan and Jason and the night he had died, and the fact that both nights had one man in common.

She looked around the living space of her home and decided she would spend the remainder of the day cleaning up. She let the place go into chaos ever since Angela's death and didn't have the energy to do anything about it. She started with the living room, purposely staying away from the bedroom as it reminded her of the last time she'd been in there with Ethan. Had she been so blinded by her history with him, her attraction to him this entire time? Her heart vehemently denied it, telling her he was not a murderer. He would never hurt anybody. But he'd been there that night. He'd been there before her, and he hadn't said a word about it. What's more, before they escorted Ethan out, Cross and Sayres said he took video footage from the hotel.

She was driving herself insane with these thoughts and decided it was best to put on some music and continue cleaning and organizing her home. Afterwards, she could prepare to return to work at the DA's office. But lately, work didn't seem to motivate her as it used to. She was no longer sulking over the lost position at Becker and Reynolds, but she was still not excited about being an ADA. But if she turned in her two weeks' notice tomorrow, what would she do? Move to another city and start over? She'd considered the possibility of relocating shortly after Jason's death but chalked it up to an impulsive decision during what was supposed to be a mourning period. Was this another one of those moments? Was she just feeling sorry for herself because her sister had just passed, her relationship with her father was non-existent, and she and Ethan...

She and Ethan what? There was no "she and Ethan," at least there couldn't be. There were too many lies, too many secrets between them. Yes, he made her crazy with wanting him whenever he touched her, but that was nothing to build a relationship from.

Sophie attacked the pile of mail lying on the coffee table and began sorting through bills and ads. It surprised, gladdened, and scared her to hear how Ethan had felt about her. She should have said something, anything, like how she'd been attracted to him, too, but felt so guilty about it. Whatever faults Jason had, he'd still been her husband, and in the beginning, she'd been in love with him. But ever since that evening at the restaurant when he introduced Ethan as his new partner, those old schoolgirl feelings she thought were long buried had resurfaced and blossomed into ripe, full-grown-woman feelings. Still, she managed to keep them tucked away out of respect and loyalty to her husband.

Her rote movements of tossing mail into two piles were halted when she came to a plain white envelope with her name and address written in her sister's handwriting. She turned the letter over but didn't find a return address. She checked the postmark and noticed the date. It had been mailed just two days before Angela had died. Sophie had a bad habit of not checking her mail every day, and upon threat from the mail carrier that he would stop delivering her mail, she cleaned out her mailbox the day after she was attacked by Josh Carelli and returned home from her father's house. However, she simply tossed everything on the coffee table without looking through any of it.

Her fingers began shaking as she gripped the letter opener, tore open the envelope, and pulled out the sheet of paper inside. What would Angela send her, and why hadn't she just texted her if she wanted to tell her something?

Sophie had her answer the second she unfolded the paper and read what was written. Angela would never text her secrets.

Archie.

CHAPTER TWENTY-SIX

"I didn't realize the case was still underway," Rebecca Johnson said, as she led Ethan through the two-story home and into the kitchen.

"I still have a few questions," Ethan said. "Just some loose ends I want to tie up before I file my report and officially close the case."

Carl Johnson's older sister, Rebecca, was a bubbly woman. She seemed to age beautifully and Ethan suspected it was because she never stopped smiling. Even though they were discussing the death of her brother and his family, Rebecca continued to maintain a natural pleasant expression.

"Did you have a chance to speak with your brother before he died?" he asked.

"You mean before he shot himself," she said and nodded her head. "I came by the house a lot after the trial to see how he was getting along. I didn't like the thought of him in here all alone in mourning. Vanessa, of course, had moved out by then. There was no way their marriage could survive after what he suspected, not to mention that scandal with the police Sergeant. Still, I tried to get Carl to come out on drives with me, but he seemed content to stay in that house with the curtains shut.

"There was nothing I could say or do, so I suggested he get some grief counseling. The last time I saw him, he promised me he would." The pleasantness in her face dipped slightly, and he guessed she was remembering the last time she saw her brother. "I never would have thought he'd do that to himself or Vanessa."

Ethan remained quiet, allowing her a moment of peace. Then, she sighed heavily and gestured to a door just off the kitchen.

"Everything of theirs will be in the cellar," she said. "I haven't had the heart to throw anything away. I've been staying here out of sentimental reasons, too. I know I could put it on the market and get a great price for it, but that would feel like giving away the last of Carl and Matthew."

He'd made the decision to visit the Johnson home the moment he sat in that interview room with Hailey and Noah. He'd told them everything that happened the night he followed Angela to her hotel room. He'd wanted answers. He wanted the name of her source. He wanted her help in getting Internal Affairs off his back. He also wanted to know why she'd stopped returning his calls, texts, or emails. They'd shared a few drinks, laughs, and he'd opened up to her about the trial, Jason, and even his feelings for Sophie. She'd said she believed him, that she knew he would never kill anyone, but then she seemed to stop all contact. Then, weeks later, he heard through the grapevine about a story being written about Jason's murder and how he was murdered by one of his own. Yes, he had been livid, because he believed Angela had taken his trust and his words and tossed them back in his face. She was writing a story about him, exposing him as Jason's killer. He had to find her, but when he visited Sophie at her office that afternoon, she'd stonewalled him, refusing to give him any information about Angela or what she was up to. So, he did something he only did with criminals—he followed Angela. He didn't know where she lived, but he knew she worked at the *San Francisco Chronicle*, and he waited there until she left work. When she left work that evening, she didn't go home, but straight toward Franklin Hotel.

But what led him to be here at the Johnson home and telling a white lie to Carl's sister was the last thing he remembered Angela saying to him, just before he left:

"You don't get it do you? This isn't just about you. This story, this whole fucking mess is one year in the making."

He'd dismissed her words and didn't remember them until his interview this morning, and it got his mind spinning. One year in the making? The only thing he could think of that involved him a year ago was the trial.

"The boxes should be easy to find," Rebecca said. "I kept everything organized on the off chance the day came I finally decide to sell this house."

Ethan thanked her and opened the cellar door, which made an audible creak. To his right was a light switch that illuminated the room. He descended the stairs and instantly spotted the cardboard boxes stacked neatly side to side. Fortunately, everything was labeled in black marker. He bypassed the ones that read *Clothing, Linen* and *Dishes*, stopped at a box labeled *Important Documents* and pulled it from its place. He didn't know what he hoped to find, but figured this was a good place to start.

* * *

Sophie cursed as the sound of Ethan's voicemail picked up once again. Where the hell was he? Was he deliberately ignoring her calls? If he wanted to be upset with her, he could wait until after she gave him Angela's story. Then the thought struck her that he could have been arrested. Maybe Sergeants Cross and Sayres finally had enough to make a conviction. Either way, she was on her own.

She threw her cell down onto the passenger seat beside her and concentrated on the slick, wet road ahead. It had begun raining earlier that morning, and the downpour had yet to let up. She needed to get to her father's house fast, but this weather was slowing her down.

She cursed her luck for not having looked at her mail or figuring any of this out sooner. Her father and Cynthia had told her Angela came to visit them a week before she died. They said she was so excited about a story that was going to make her career. It was the story everyone had been looking for, the story everyone assumed Sophie knew about. She'd been questioned by the police, her colleagues at work, and even outright attacked in an alley for it, because no one could believe Angela wouldn't tell her sister where to find it. And they had all been right. Angela *had* told her—Angela had whispered it to her.

She was winding the hillside now that would take her to her father's house. Glancing into her rearview mirror, she felt her heart speed up as she saw a car coming up behind her. Ethan! He must have gotten her message. Thank God, he hadn't been arrested. The truth was well within their grasp, and what Angela had left for her was either going to remove all suspicion from him as a killer or expose him as one.

She looked into the rearview mirror at the car tailing her. What the hell? It was coming up to her fast. She frowned, feeling the little hairs on the back of her neck rise. He's going to hit me. That was dangerous on this narrow, wet road, and Ethan knew that. Why would he…

Her eyes widened. She could see clearly in the rearview mirror now that the car was so close, and the moment she recognized the face, she felt herself thrown forward in her seat. Instinctively, she hit the brakes, and the car skidded forward and began to fishtail. Sophie tried to steady her breathing, desperate to get the car under control, but she was rammed from behind again. This time, her car lurched to the side, dangerously close to the edge of the two-lane road. Sophie screamed, knowing she was running out of time. She tried one last attempt to straighten the wheel and get her tires on even ground, but the car behind her was too fast, and her assailant could guess her every move.

One final crash into her rear bumper and Sophie's car went over the edge. She was careening down the hill, coming fast upon a bank of trees. Sophie braced for the impact. She only felt the first instant jolt when her car hit the immovable tree, and then, nothing at all.

* * *

"This is everything else from the basement I could find. I showed these pictures to that journalist, too, but she didn't find them to be too interesting," Rebecca said, handing him the stack of photo albums. "She said she had all the photos of the family she needed from the trial."

"What did interest her?" Ethan said, opening the first album.

"She wanted to know about Carl and Vanessa's personal lives, mainly. She said it would give the story some substance if she was able to personalize it. She especially wanted to know about their lives before they were married. You know, past relationships and things like that."

"I couldn't tell her much about Vanessa," Rebecca continued. "She and I never really got close as sisters-in-law. I guess you could say we were civil to each other for Carl's sake, and when I heard what she did to Matthew and the way she carried on with that cop, I was completely done with her. I had nothing to say about her to that reporter, but I was able to talk to her about Carl and his first marriage."

Ethan stopped when he came to a collection of baby photos and looked up at Rebecca. "His first wife didn't come to the trial. I remember conducting the investigation and running across her name, but she didn't have any relevance to the case."

Rebecca shook her head. "Well that's not surprising. She gave up her maternal rights to Matthew when he was only seven months old. Carl said she wasn't ready to be a mother, and was all too willing to let him care for the baby while she went off and 'found herself.'"

She made air quotes with her finger before rolling her eyes heavenward.

"Did you ever meet her?" Ethan asked, returning to the baby photos, and noticed one picture in the bottom right hand corner that gave him pause.

"Once or twice while she and Carl were dating. This was long before they were married. She was in the military then."

She must have noticed him studying the picture intently, because she leaned forward and smiled. "That's Matthew when he just turned three."

Ethan knew who it was, but couldn't figure out why the picture bothered him so much. Maybe he'd seen it sometime during the trial. There had been plenty of baby pictures of Matthew circulating in the newspapers and online every day, outraging the public even more that no one had yet put the baby killer, Vanessa Johnson, away for the rest of her life.

His cell phone buzzed in his pocket. He pulled it out and looked at the display. Sophie. He also saw he had one voice-mail message, probably from her too. He texted a quick message saying he'd call her back when he was done with his interview.

"He gave her a copy of that photograph," Rebecca said. "In fact, he sent her a lot of photos over the years. I guess they eventually melted her heart, because she came to see Carl one day, asking for a chance to come back into her son's life."

"Who came back?" Ethan asked.

"Laura. Matthew's mother."

"What did Carl say?"

"He was hesitant about it. He said it would be good for Matthew to know his biological mother, but it might be confusing, considering he only knew Vanessa as his mother. You see, by that time Carl had remarried, and Vanessa had adopted the boy as her own."

Ethan decided it was time to wrap this up. He'd think about the photograph later. Right now, he was interested in what Sophie had to say to him.

"I appreciate you talking to me. You wouldn't happen to know where I could find Laura Johnson now, would you?"

Rebecca's face brightened. "I do now, thanks to that pretty journalist. It's such a shame about what happened to her. Anyway, I told her I wanted to meet up with Laura to see if she wanted a few of Matthew's things before I donated them to the group homes, but I didn't know where to find her. Ms. James said she would do her best to try and track her down, and she did."

"Where is she?" Ethan reached for his cell phone and chose the memo option, ready to write the address down.

"She's working for the police," Rebecca said, "and apparently, she goes by her middle name now. Hailey."

CHAPTER TWENTY-SEVEN

"*E*than, it's me. Meet me at my father's house as soon as you get this. I know where Angie's story is."

Ethan punched the *end* button as he cursed the traffic moving across the wet Oakland Bay Bridge. He next dialed the number for the precinct.

"Homicide, Sergeant Sayres speaking."

"Noah, it's Ethan."

"Ethan, where the hell are you? Your lawyer arrived and so has IAD. You were supposed to be here for your second interview twenty minutes ago."

"Never mind that," Ethan snapped. "Where's Cross?"

"She's out looking for you. Look, don't do this. Come in peacefully, and we can get this over with."

Ethan swore. "If she comes back, I want her put in custody."

Silence, and then Noah erupted. "What? For what?"

"Suspicion of two murders. Look I don't have time to explain right now. Just spread the word that Sergeant Hailey Cross is being sought for questioning. I want her brought in now."

"Are you fucking crazy? You're the one who's under suspicion for two murders. Nobody is going to bring her in just on your say so. Have you ever heard of evidence? Get your ass over here, now!"

"I'm on my way to get you some evidence," he said and ended the call.

He next tried dialing Sophie's number to let her know he was on his way, but the call went straight to voicemail. His gut told him something wasn't right, and it already made him nervous that he didn't know Hailey's whereabouts.

It seemed to take ages to get across the bridge, but after a few miles of navigating the turns on the winding hillside, he had to slow down.

"What the hell," he muttered.

Several police and emergency vehicles lined the side of the road, but he couldn't see any cars indicating there had been an accident. Maybe a body, he thought to himself, and driven only by pure instinct, he pulled his car over to the shoulder and got out. The rain was still coming down strong as he used his jacket for a shield and ran over to the police vehicles.

"I'm Sergeant Markham with the SFPD. What happened?"

The officer on duty motioned down the hill to a car smashed into a tree. "Somebody lost control of their vehicle. This is third accident I've been called to since my shift started. This rain isn't agreeing with people. Hey!"

Ethan ignored him as soon as he recognized the car and hurried down the embankment, half running, half sliding in the muddy terrain, with his heart hammering in his chest. He shoved the EMTs away and looked inside the car, ready to pull her out himself. But no one was there.

"Where is she?" he demanded. "What hospital did they take her to?"

He started to hurry back up the hill to his car, realizing

the closest hospital was San Francisco General, but one of the officers grabbed his arm.

"Hold on for a minute. You know who this vehicle belongs to, sir?"

Ethan yanked his arm free. "Sophia James. She's an ADA for San Francisco County." The sight of her purse lying on the passenger floor with all of its contents strewn about, confirmed it.

"Her wallet is right there," Ethan said. "I'm sure her license and registration are in there. I need to go find her."

"Well when you do, let us know," the officer stated dryly.

That gave him pause. "Excuse me?"

He shrugged and continued. "We figured the car was stolen. Sure, it's registered to Ms. James, but I couldn't tell you if she was driving it or not. When we arrived on scene, the driver side door was wide open and no one was inside."

* * *

One month earlier…

"You told me a lot about the trial and everything leading up to it," Angela said. "But you seem to avoid talking about everything that happened afterwards."

"You can find that in the papers, too," he said. "Carl killed his wife and then himself."

"No, I meant everything between you and Jason."

He fell silent.

"You never talk about the night Jason died. Why?"

He sighed heavily. "I don't talk about it, because I'm still working out the details myself. I'm the prime suspect. I was the last to see him alive, but…"

He trailed off, and after a moment, Angela prodded him. "But there's more, isn't there? More that you haven't told to anyone."

He fell silent again.

"Ethan, are you there?"

"What you said in our first conversation, about everything being off the record, it still holds true, right?"

"Yes."

He took several steady breaths before continuing. "I told Jason something that night that I should have just kept to myself. By all rights, it pissed him off, but at the time, I didn't care. I was still pissed myself for the mess he made of the case, the department, and his own career. He came after me, got a few blows in, and then I—"

"Stop Ethan."

Her sudden exclamation shocked him into silence.

"What's wrong?"

"Just stop talking. Please."

"Angie, what is it?"

"I don't want to know. I don't want to know anymore."

"Angie?"

She hung up.

CHAPTER TWENTY-EIGHT

*E*than swore a blue streak when he saw the front door was ajar. It was barely four in the afternoon, but with the thunder clouds, fog, and rain, it looked much darker and more ominous. With his gun and flashlight leading him, he stepped onto the front porch. He wrapped twice on the door with the barrel and called out.

"Mr. James. This is Sergeant Ethan Markham with the police. Your door is open, sir. Is everyone okay in there?"

Silence.

"Mr. James, can you hear me? Mrs. James? Sophie?"

No response.

"I'm going to kick the door open with my foot. If you can hear me, keep your hands where I can see them."

He slowly edged the door open with the toe of his shoe and positioned himself on one side of the door frame. Angling his head, he looked inside but didn't see anyone. He slowly and quietly entered the house, checking behind the door. He then moved along the walls toward the staircase. Before he could yell upstairs, he heard movement coming from the dining room and whipped his gun and flashlight toward the sound.

"Come out, slowly, showing me your hands," he ordered, but no one appeared.

"Do it now!"

Several agonizing seconds passed before he saw the figures of both Larry and Cynthia James with their hands raised slowly come into view of his flashlight. Ethan tensed. Right behind them was the barrel of a gun gripped by one steady hand.

"Where's your backup?" Hailey asked.

Ethan kept his gun trained on her without wavering. "You know me, I like to fly solo."

"Not very smart, Sergeant."

He shrugged. "I've got a lot of questions for you, and you obviously need to explain yourself, so how about you let him and his wife go, and we can talk this out alone."

She smiled genuinely. "Is that really the best you've got? You know, I've always liked you, Ethan, and you have to believe I never wanted to involve you in any of this. But because of your negligence and refusing to see what was going on in front of you, you let that baby killer go free."

"Your son's killer," he countered softly.

"Don't you dare try to be my friend." She poked the gun into Larry James's head. "All of this is because of you, Jason, and that ADA bitch who threw away that trial. The three of you let that murderer go free!"

Ethan kept his gun on her. There was nothing to say to that, and he didn't want to risk Larry and Cynthia's lives in this showdown with her.

"Your fight is with me, so why are you involving Sophie's parents in this?"

"Because Angela is dead, but I still need that story, and

I'm betting her father knows where his daughter kept her top-secret exclusive story."

"I told you I don't know where it is—" Larry began, but before he could finish his plea, Hailey swung her arm and the barrel of the gun hit him in the head with enough force to bring him to his knees.

"Larry," Cynthia screamed.

Ethan moved in slowly and kept his tone low and even, despite the urge to rush at her and overpower her. "Leave them out of this. No one knows where that story is, and why the hell do you care?"

"Because she tricked me," Hailey snarled. "I was her source, Ethan. I was the reason she even had a story to begin with!"

He took a few deep breaths, trying to ignore Larry on the floor with the side of his head bleeding profusely. He needed medical attention, but Ethan had to put Hailey down first.

"You were the source? It was you who tried to frame me for Jason's death. You told Angela I killed him."

"I fed her information about a cover up and how the department was protecting you for killing your partner. I even fabricated some evidence for her," she said, and then her face had a regretful look. "I didn't want to kill you, Ethan. I just wanted revenge. You and Jason were partners and frankly, you should have known what he was doing and done something to stop it. He deserved to die. Because of him and his wandering dick, that woman got away with killing my son."

"It was a mistrial, Hailey," he said, trying to keep his tone calm. "If you could've just held on a little longer, we could have brought her up on charges again. Why didn't you just come to me?"

"No! It was over. The department was a laughing stock, no jury was going to take any evidence coming from us seriously now that one of our own was having an affair with a murder defendant. No prosecutor would take the risk, including your little girlfriend, Sophie. I had to handle it myself. As the kids like to call it, I would get my own street justice."

Ethan took another glance at Larry, whose head was now lulled to the side, and then back to Hailey who seemed to go into a daze as memories surrounded her.

"I heard you and Jason arguing that night, you know. I followed you to his apartment building and waited in the corridor. The walls in that cheap building were paper thin. You were so angry. For a moment, I wanted to go in there and applaud you for the way you let him have it. Then I heard your confession about Sophie."

She paused, shaking her head and chuckling. "Shame on you, Ethan. You never told me the two of you were summer sweethearts. That explains a lot. Anyway, I heard the two of you fighting, then nothing. At first, I thought you killed him, yourself, especially when you came out of that apartment, breathing fire. I ducked around the corner and stayed there until I was sure you left the building. Then, I went to Jason's door. I gently turned the knob, let myself in, and he was there, still on the floor, nursing his bloody nose. He didn't see or hear me enter, but when I walked up to him, he said: 'Did you come back for more?'

"I raised my gun to his head and said: 'No. You've done enough, asshole.' And just as he looked up at me…"

She trailed off, staring at a blank space on the wall, reliving that night, and Ethan took advantage of that moment to move in just an inch closer.

"I called the cops as a concerned citizen, told them I heard gunshots and gave them your description."

"But you couldn't end it there," Ethan said. "You had to kill the woman who was going to help you get your revenge."

Hailey kept the gun leveled at his heart. He was almost within arm's reach to knock it out of her hands.

"I don't know at what point Angela started to suspect me," she said. "I was her source and suddenly, she began to investigate me. When I asked her about her progress with the story, she kept giving me the same bullshit line: 'It's coming along.' Then, she stopped answering my phone calls and texts, and I knew something was wrong. When I got a call from Rebecca, Carl's sister, she told me a black woman, a reporter, visited her, asking questions about me. I knew then I had to get rid of Angela."

"Hailey—"

"But Jason and Vanessa deserved the worst," she said, still lost in her memories. "I visited Carl, comforted him, and we cried together for our son. Then I used his grief and anger to convince him to do away with that bitch!"

She stopped, and as she stared at him, he noticed tears welling in her blue eyes.

"I never expected him to kill himself, but I underestimated just how much pain he was going through." She aimed the gun for Ethan's head, her face a mask of rage. "That's the only thing I'm sorry about."

"What about leaving your son when he was a baby? Are you sorry about that, too?"

"Shut up!"

"Face it, Hailey. You abandoned that boy to a monster. If anyone is to blame, it's you."

She came forward, keeping the gun aimed at his face. "You don't know what the hell you're talking about."

"I think I do. I had a nice long chat with your former sister-in-law, too. All these killings, Carl's suicide, it could have all been prevented if you'd given the least amount of shit to see your child. Now, you want to come and try to clean up the damage all in the name of revenge? You may have killed Jason out of revenge and convinced Carl to do the same, but what about Angela and Joshua Carelli? That was no longer about Matthew. You killed them to protect yourself. You're still that selfish woman who left your son all those years ago."

The barrel of the gun slammed into his head in two quick successions. He dropped to his knees, but was determined to stay conscious. He heard Cynthia cry out, but Ethan didn't move or say anything, determined to keep Hailey's attention on him. He'd rather she come after him than hurt Sophie's parents. He also wanted to keep her talking and distracted because from behind her, he could see the faintest of movements.

Someone was in the kitchen.

* * *

Sophie made it all the way upstairs without a sound and thanked God for the set of carpeted stairs leading from the kitchen. She paused at the top, listening for voices and nursing her bruised side. Hailey was still talking, and Sophie prayed Ethan could keep her talking until she could get her hands on a weapon. Maybe then the two of them could overpower Hailey. She continued on to her and Angela's bedroom, which was directly above the living room. One misstep and she would be found out. If Hailey knew she was up there, she would no doubt turn her wrath toward Ethan and her parents. She needed to move fast.

As soon as she entered the room, she spotted the telephone on the nightstand separating the two full-sized beds. She picked it up and nearly slammed it down in disgust before remembering her stay quiet rule. No dial tone.

"Shit," she hissed.

She turned toward the window to see the sky darkening

175

outside. Thunder crackled as though mocking her. She prayed Ethan had called for backup before coming into the house. She crouched beside her bed and winced at the ache in her knees and lower back. Either she was going to the hospital or going home to take a long hot shower when this was all over. The air bag in her car had deployed, saving her from hitting the windshield when her car slammed against the tree. She'd been dazed on impact but thankfully still conscious. At first, she'd worried that her assailant would come down to make sure she was dead, but she remained alone in the car, shivering from the cold rain, the wind chill, and fear.

Focus, Sophie, she told herself and stuck her hand inside the mattress. She didn't feel anything, but it had to be there. Reaching as far as her arm would go, she desperately felt around, looking to grasp something and finally, there it was.

As soon as her fingers gripped the paper, she yanked it out. It was a small manila envelope made bulky by the object inside. She opened it and tipped it over into her palm. Even as the room grew darker by the minute, she could see the object clear enough to know it was a small flash drive. As her heart began to race, Sophie tucked it into her back pocket and headed for the closet. Inside, she grabbed hold of a heavy wooden bat. At the same instant, a scream came from downstairs. Sophie moved quietly to the hallway.

CHAPTER TWENTY-NINE

*H*e sensed more than saw the figure creeping along the wall, trying her best to stay hidden.

Sophie.

Ethan wanted to wring her neck. He suspected it had been her in the kitchen, but didn't want to believe she would do anything so reckless. But knowing Sophie, there was no way she'd wait patiently outside with her family in danger. He had to keep Hailey talking.

"I made a remark that night of Angela's death about you wearing makeup. I don't think I've ever seen you in makeup. You had to cover up the scratch marks from Angela."

"Bravo," Hailey said, dryly. "But a little too late. I had to take the time to clean her fingernails."

Ethan wiped blood from his temple and started to slowly rise to his feet with his hands up.

"Careful," Hailey warned, keeping her gun steady and trained on him.

"You killed that kid because he was your witness?"

"I followed Angela for weeks, waiting for my opportunity

to get rid of her. Then I saw she moved in to the Franklin Hotel for three days. Something told me it was her place to hide out once the story broke. It was like kismet when I found out Carelli worked there. He was a snitch from day one. He worked for coke, and I promised to keep his problem-ass out of jail if he made me a duplicate of her hotel room key and kept watch."

She paused to mumble a few curses and insults about Carelli. "It turns out he was a double snitch, playing both Angela and me. I had no idea she paid him to let her know when I walked in the hotel. Then you broke his nose and he got himself thrown in jail. Sophie did me a favor by dropping the charges against him. It gave me a chance to get him out of the way, too."

He tried again to reason with her. "Let them go, Hailey. We can go back to the station and look for the story together. These people don't know where it is. If there even is a story, the department will find it, consider it bad publicity and shut it down before it even gets started. No one else has to die."

She made a sad face. "Too bad you didn't give me that speech about forty-five minutes ago, before I plowed your ADA girlfriend's car down an embankment and into a tree."

"Sophie," Larry groaned from the floor.

"Shut up," Hailey said. "She had it coming, too. If your little girl hadn't been so focused on her dream job, she would have noticed Vanessa Johnson gearing up to make her look like a fool in her own house and the courtroom!"

Wherever you are, get the hell out of here. Ethan needed so badly for Sophie to hear those words going through his head, but as the lightning illuminated the sky, he spotted her shadow just for an instant getting closer to Hailey's back, keeping a firm grip on whatever weapon she held in her hand. But even though she had been married to one, he knew

Sophie didn't know or even understand a cop's instincts. She was playing a dangerous game and underestimating Hailey. If she turned around and saw her, Sophie would be dead.

He knew the moment Hailey paused in her words and her eyes dawned with realization that she knew, and they were all out of time.

She whipped around, and in a flash, her gun was aimed directly at Sophie. At the same time, Ethan pounced, fearing he was already too late.

* * *

Sophie's heart stopped when Hailey pivoted toward her. But she couldn't allow that gun to be pointed in her face, so recalling her softball days, she swung the bat with all she had. It struck Hailey in the shoulder with a satisfying thud. Hailey cried out, but didn't go down. She kept her gun raised and managed to fire off a single shot just as Ethan tackled her to the ground.

"I just want justice for my son, Ethan," Hailey cried out from underneath him. "Get off of me, goddammit!"

The house was nearly shrouded in darkness now. Sophie could hear scurrying about as her father untied her step-mother. She then heard the two of them calling her as they rushed over to her. She tried to tell them she was all right, and that's when she felt the rush of pain and realized for the first time she was on the ground. She touched the spot where the pain was burning and came away with fingers soaked in blood. Hailey was still screaming and cursing, but Ethan kept her restrained while barking orders into his cell phone and keeping his eyes on Sophie. She tried to focus on him and then her father, but the pain was too unbearable, and she could no longer keep her eyes open. She was falling into darkness again. The accident had been instant, but this time, she was registering the people around her whom she loved and who loved her, and was desperate not to leave them. She wanted to cling to reality, but the warm, enveloping fingers of unconsciousness were so tempting. The pain would be gone if she just closed her eyes.

CHAPTER THIRTY

Sophie could sense him the moment he walked into the hospital room. She looked up and regarded him with caution in her eyes, unsure of what he wanted to say to her. He seemed to be staring at her the same way.

The nurse, oblivious to the tension that suddenly filled the air, continued fluffing the pillows behind Sophie's back.

"How does that feel?" she asked.

Sophie nodded and nearly asked for something else mundane that the nurse could do for her, realizing she suddenly didn't want to be alone with Ethan, but the young woman had already turned around, saw him, and smiled.

She then turned back to Sophie with a wink and whispered. "He's been here ever since you were brought in, pacing the hallways."

Sophie could only smile. That didn't mean anything. Ethan cared for her, that much she knew, so of course he'd wait to see that she was okay. But she didn't want him here just to give her a pat on the back with a job well done.

Ethan watched as the nurse left, closing the door behind

her, and then turned to Sophie. "I spoke to your father. I'm glad to hear his wounds were minor."

She smiled. "He and Cynthia have been here every day making sure they know my release day. I think they're afraid I'll go back to that empty house alone."

"You have a wound that nearly damaged your kidneys," Ethan said. "I'm going to make sure you don't go back to that house alone, either."

She quickly changed the subject, growing uncomfortable from the care in his tone. "Sergeant Cross?"

He cleared his throat and stepped forward. "She's been taken into custody."

"Has she said anything?"

"Other than what she told me at your father's house, she's been quiet. I guess when she realized she wasn't going to get away with more murder, she wised up and got a lawyer."

Sophie looked away.

He stepped closer to her bed. "What's the matter?"

She hesitated a moment and then looked at him. "I guess I just feel sorry for her. She did all of this because she was a grieving mother."

"Unfortunately, other mothers lose their children, Sophie. They don't start murdering people because of it."

"I know. I know. But listening to her talk, I felt responsible. If I had—"

"If you had what? What could you have possibly done to keep that trial from ending in any other way?"

"I don't know, but maybe I could've done something."

"She killed your husband."

She looked at him again and honestly didn't know what to say to that. She didn't want to tell him the ugly truth that there were times when things got so bad between them, she wished Jason wouldn't come home. That every time the doorbell rang, she wanted it to be a couple of police officers telling her that he'd been in some terrible accident or that he'd been shot on the job. Those were her lowest days. How could she tell this man that long before Jason died, she'd stopped loving him and when the day finally came that two officers showed up at her doorstep, she'd felt nothing?

"It doesn't stop me from feeling sorry for her."

He nodded. "I understand."

Suddenly, she jerked, nearly forgetting the entire reason they were in this mess. "The flash drive! I put it in my back jeans pocket before I came downstairs."

She motioned to the pile of clothes folded neatly in a corner chair. Ethan went to her jeans and retrieved the small flash drive. He held it up with a question in his eyes.

"Angie's story. The real story in which she exposes Hailey. That was what she'd been so excited about. She must have realized that her source was the actual murderer and began investigating her. Hailey found out about it, but not before Angie could finish her story."

"How did you find it?" he asked.

She explained to him the little game she and Angela used to play as kids when they wanted to keep secrets between them.

Ethan laughed and shook his head. "Betty and Veronica."

Then his smile faded as he looked down at the flash drive. When he locked eyes with her again, his face was serious. "You were looking for it that night in the hotel room."

It wasn't a question, so she didn't say anything.

"You were looking for it to destroy it."

"Ethan—"

"Because you thought there was a chance I might have killed Jason."

"That's not true."

"It is." He stepped closer to the bed. "I've been trying to get you alone since his death to tell you what happened that night, but you've avoided me. Now, I'm going to talk, and you're going to listen."

* * *

As soon as Ethan entered the apartment, he could feel this visit was going to be miles different from the last time he came to see Jason. As soon as he walked in the door, there was an elephant standing between the two of them, and neither seemed to be too eager to get rid of it.

Without asking, Jason handed Ethan a bottled beer and motioned for him to sit on the sofa, while Jason chose an armchair opposite him. Ethan wanted to refuse the beer and tell Jason he'd had more than enough himself, but he accepted it without a word and sat. Jason was leaning forward in the chair, his elbows resting on his knees, and his beer cradled between his hands. He looked to be in a daze, and Ethan followed his line of sight to what lay before him on the coffee table. The San Francisco Chronicle *was there with a black, bold headline that read: Johnson Trial Ends in Murder / Suicide. Ethan didn't have to pick it up. He'd seen the headlines everywhere but had been made aware by his colleagues that Carl Johnson shot and killed his wife with a .38 and then put it to his head. Their bodies now lay resting in the morgue, waiting for an autopsy and then ultimately, next of kin.*

He looked up at Jason who was shaking his head. Anger and sadness seemed to wrestle for first place in his eyes. Finally, he turned away from the newspaper and also from memories, it seemed.

"What a fucking mess," he grumbled.

Ethan didn't argue with him. He wanted to tell him it was a mess Jason, himself, had partly caused, but he was never one to kick a man while he was down. Instead, he steered the conversation to his career.

"Any news on when your suspension will be lifted?"

Jason shrugged and finally took a drink of his own beer. "My union rep can't give me a definite answer. The lieutenant and the rest of the big brass seem to be dragging their feet, but I can't blame them. I'm sure when I do get back, I'll need to meet with the department psychiatrist and check in with IAD every minute of every day."

"At least you'll have your job back."

"Yeah, but without a partner." Jason let that gauntlet lie resting between them and pierced Ethan with narrowed eyes. "Have they assigned you any one yet?"

"No."

"I want you to know, I don't resent or blame you for making that decision. I'm a pariah over there now. You need to look out for yourself."

Anger slowly simmered inside of Ethan. "You think I requested a new partner because of your reputation?"

"Yeah, I do."

"Then fuck you!" His tone was low, hard, and vibrating with fury. "I requested another partner, because you didn't trust me enough to let me know what the hell was going on. If you had told me you were sleeping with that woman—"

"You would've told me to come forward," Jason interrupted.

"For the good of our case," Ethan fired back. "If you admitted what was happening, we could've done something about it. There wouldn't have been a mistrial, and I wouldn't be left holding my dick in my hands!"

He noticed Jason's grip on his bottle tighten, but he surged on.

"Look up the meaning of partner one day while you're sitting here on suspension and feeling sorry for yourself. Trust me, you won't find it says to betray your own partner, your department or your wife."

Jason stood. "You can never keep her out of this. Every chance you get, you throw in my face what I did to Sophie, well save it.

That horse is dead, and just in case you have any plans to pick up where I left off, you should know she'll never leave me."

Ethan also stood. It was now time to get rid of the elephant. "Why are you telling me this?"

Jason's face changed to a sneer. "You think I'm stupid? You think I don't know what I walked in on that night? You could cut the tension between you two with a knife."

He swiped up the beer bottle, took several deep gulps, wiped his mouth, and then turned and hurled the bottle at the wall. He then turned and faced Ethan with rage in his eyes, but Ethan didn't move.

"Tell me the truth. Did you fuck my wife?"

"No. I met Sophie and fell in love with her long before she was your wife."

Ethan braced himself, watching and waiting for Jason to make his move. He was fuming, and Ethan knew his partner would not waste time.

Jason moved in and swung his fist to the side of Ethan's face, but because of his intoxication, his move was delayed, sloppy. Ethan ducked and then shoved Jason away from him.

"You're drunk. Go to bed and sleep it off."

Jason charged again, this time going for a left jab to his nose. Ethan blocked with his right and followed up with a punch to his side. He didn't put too much power in it, but just enough to disarm Jason.

"I'm not going to fight you, dammit!"

But he knew Jason was seeing red and not listening to reason. He ducked his head and charged for Ethan's gut. Ethan turned to the side and trapped Jason's head in a chokehold. Jason swung wildly with his fists, trying to break the hold, but Ethan kept firm.

"I'm sorry," Ethan said. "I never should've told you that."

Jason kept swinging.

"I'm sorry," he said, again and kept saying it until he felt Jason

growing weak. He released him instantly and stepped back. Jason bent over at the knees, coughing and gagging.

Ethan went to the small kitchen, opened the refrigerator and spied a bottle of water. He untwisted the cap and handed it to Jason, who took it and drank the cold liquid down greedily.

When he took enough gulps to soothe his throat, he lowered the bottle and looked to Ethan.

"You're a son of a bitch. You never said anything before. I introduced you two, and all this time, there was a history between you."

"I didn't think it was my place. I left the choice to tell you up to her, but she didn't want to. I guess you two are used to keeping secrets from each other."

"What the hell do you know about our marriage?"

"Enough to know that it's fucked up!"

"Get out."

They glared at one another for a long time, knowing this was the end of more than just a career partnership. Ethan turned, grabbed his jacket on the chair, and let himself out.

"I left," Ethan said. "I left him, and he was still alive. That's what I told IAD." He came closer to her bed and lowered his voice. "What I didn't tell them, Sophie…"

Her head was bent low the entire time he'd been talking. She was steadily picking at her fingernails, and when he paused, she finally looked up, her eyes filled with guilt and regret.

"You didn't tell them that you saw me."

* * *

Ethan left the apartment, not listening to the barrage of names Jason hurled at his back. He slammed the door behind him, turned and jogged down the steps to the first floor, and shoved the security door open, letting the night air hit him in the face. The chill would do him good in cooling down his hot temper. He knew this part of town and decided it would be safe enough to take a quick walk around the block before he got into his car and drove home.

What the fuck had he been thinking to confess his love for Sophie like that? Confess his love for another man's wife? What had been the point? If the situation had been reversed, he would have gone on the offensive too and attacked. But Jason had been drunk, so it would not have been a fair fight, and Ethan knew he had no right to fight him in the first place. He would go see him in a couple of days when they both calmed down and sit and talk it out, and Ethan would apologize again, and vow to never come near Sophie again.

Ethan zipped his jacket up to his chin and dug his hands in his pockets as he began the short walk around the block. He didn't want to think about how the sudden absence of her out of his life would feel, because it would only make him think about that summer and how she'd made the choice to end things between them as soon as fall began, and she returned to school. She hadn't given him any choice in the matter but made the decision for the both of them. He could only go along with what she wanted and deal with the absence of her. Just like now. But now was much different. She belonged to another man, and he wasn't going to come between that.

He turned the corner, and when he looked up, he saw his car in the distance. He looked around and realized he almost completed the walk around the block, and although he'd gotten his temper under control, he was still feeling frustrated. But he would just have to find a way to deal with those feelings and move on with his life.

As he came closer to his car, he noticed a figure in a dark wool coat walking quickly and purposefully to Jason's apartment building. It was a woman wearing a black wool hat that covered her short cropped hair. When she glanced around, Ethan caught a glimpse of her in profile and recognized the smooth cocoa-colored skin of the woman he couldn't stop thinking about.

Sophie.

She was laying her hand on the buzzer to the security door, and Ethan wanted to tell her he'd left Jason in a sour mood but told himself she could handle her own husband, and it wasn't any of his business. She kept ringing the bell, and as Ethan got closer, he heard the sound of the buzzer going off, granting her entry.

Get in the car and go home.

His keys were in his hand, and he was walking to his car but still had Sophie in his sights. He looked at her as she pulled open the security door. He unlocked his car door, watching as she stepped inside and the door was closing behind her. He couldn't help himself.

"Sophie!"

He didn't know why he called out to her. He didn't know what he wanted to say to her. He didn't know why he couldn't just leave her be, why he couldn't just leave the two of them to whatever screwed-up marriage they wanted, why he couldn't just let her go.

She turned just as the door closed, and he saw her face through the slightly darkened window pane. He stepped from around his car and moved toward the door where she waited on the other side. Then she did something that caused him to come to a complete stop. She raised a black gloved hand and placed it against the window pane, like a traffic cop signaling a car to stop. Then she shook her head and mouthed the word "Go."

She then turned and he watched as she ran up the stairs to the second floor. To Jason.

* * *

The hospital room was so quiet as the two of them relived that night. Finally, Sophie swiped furiously at her tears and exhaled.

"I went there to tell him I wanted a divorce. I was tired of tiptoeing around the subject. The marriage had been over long before Vanessa Johnson, and I went there to tell him so and that I wouldn't fight him for anything."

She paused before continuing. "He was dead when I got there. I saw his body on the floor. There was so much blood. I ran out of there and used my cell to call 9-1-1. Just like Hailey said, she must have killed him right after you left."

"But you didn't know that at the time. You thought I killed him."

She looked up at him, her wet eyes pleading. "I knew in my heart, you could never have done it, but he was right there, dead in front of me, and you were the last one I saw leave his building."

"And you were the last one I saw," he said. "All, this time, we were both scared that the other—"

"It's over now," she said, cutting him off. "Take the flash drive with you. Show it to IAD and get yourself cleared."

She noticed him stiffening ever so slightly. "And that's it?"

She suddenly felt the need to look everywhere else but at him. "Yes. Goodbye, Ethan."

She knew he wanted to say something to her, and she wished he would just say it, because God knew she didn't have the courage to speak any more.

He walked to the door, put his hand on the knob, and then stopped to turn around and look at her. "For over a year, I've been carrying around this guilt for leaving Jason vulnerable to a killer, for still loving his wife, and for thinking that if only he weren't around, I could have you again."

Sophie looked away embarrassed and chilled that his words echoed her own thoughts.

"I'm done feeling guilt. I'm done with it all. See you around, Sophie."

With that, he turned and left her room without looking back.

CHAPTER THIRTY-ONE

"How did you put it together?" Noah asked, dropping a file on Ethan's desk. "How did you know it was Hailey?"

Ethan looked up from his cluttered desk. "Matthew's picture. I remember seeing it in Hailey's badge holder. It was one they never showed in the trial, but I remember seeing it when her badge would sometimes turn backwards. She always caught it, turned it back around fast, and I never asked who the boy was."

"I did," Noah said. "She told me it was her nephew." Then he looked away and shook his head. "I had no idea she was going through all of that. I was her partner."

"Just because you work side by side with someone for years, doesn't mean you'll find out everything about them. You can still get fooled in the end."

Noah smiled sheepishly. "I guess you would know."

"What's this?" Ethan asked, picking up the manila folder and avoiding the topic of Jason, which would inevitably lead to thoughts of Sophie.

"I was going over Hailey's desk and found these phone

records. She apparently got a warrant to obtain them when we started investigating you."

"Why are you giving them to me?"

He shrugged. "I snagged these before IAD swooped down and confiscated everything on her desk. Considering everything, I thought you should have it back."

"I appreciate it," Ethan said. "I'll shred it as soon as I get home."

"Before you do that, satisfy my curiosity on something." He came around the desk, leaned down, and pointed to a series of telephone numbers. "You seemed to call this particular one a lot."

Ethan looked at the number and shrugged. "It was Angela's number. We were talking a lot over the months. She was using me as part of her story, remember?"

"No. *This* is Angela's number." Noah pointed to another number on the page. "And she called you once over a three-month period. This one right here that shows up over and over again, actually belongs to Sophia James. There's only one call from Angela's cell phone and nearly sixty to and from Sophie's cell phone."

Ethan studied the two numbers, frowned, and looked up at Noah. "You sure about that?"

"Hailey had me verify all the numbers on that page. I wondered why she seemed to be giving me legwork, but now, I see it was her way of keeping me busy while she covered her ass. Listen, it's none of my business, but if you and Sophie had something going on—"

"We didn't," Ethan said, cutting off his suspicions. "I tried calling her a few times after Jason's death to give her some support, but she didn't want to talk to me, so I left her alone." He looked down at the sheet of numbers. "At least, I thought I did."

"I'm not trying to insinuate anything," Noah said. "From

what I heard, you and Sophie only worked the Johnson trial together, and ever since then, I heard she began trading all cases with your name as primary investigator with her colleagues. These calls take place after the trial, so I only wondered." He stopped and seemed to study Ethan. "By the look on your face, you're just as confused as I am."

But Ethan wasn't confused. An answer was forming in his head that he didn't want to acknowledge, because if he did, it would mean Sophie had been lying to him for months. Suddenly, so many memories began to assault him all at once, and he could no longer deny it.

He shook his head. "That's impossible."

He'd made the comment to himself, but Noah spoke up as he headed back toward his desk. "It's all right there in black and white, but like I said, it's over now. Do what you want with it."

He thought back to the night Sophie called him, in a panic over seeing Angela's body. His phone display had come up "Angela" but he dismissed it then, assuming she must have seen her sister's phone and grabbed for it on instinct. But now with the glaring evidence that he and she had been calling each other more than he'd called Angela, well, it didn't make any sense. Unless…

And then, Sophie's words resounded crystal clear in his head.

"You told her everything, but I was your girlfriend. Did you choose the wrong girl?"

CHAPTER THIRTY-TWO

*T*hree weeks later...

She was sitting on the steps leading up to his front porch. Ethan slowed his steps, surprised to see her. They had not spoken in weeks, since he left her hospital room. But it didn't mean he stopped keeping tabs on her. He'd made daily calls to Larry and the hospital up until the day she was released, inquiring about her condition. She was healing better than expected everyone had said, and from the sight of her at his doorstep, that hadn't been exaggerated. Still, none of it explained why she came to see him after she'd made it clear she wasn't interested in seeing him anymore. But curiosity forced him to keep walking and close the distance between them.

When he reached her, she stood to greet him, and a hesitant smile broke across her face before she spoke.

"Do you mind if I come inside so we can talk?"

In response, he hoisted the bag of takeout Chinese in his hand and gestured for her to precede him to the front door. He opened it, and they climbed the single flight of stairs to the second floor in silence. Ethan kept watch, noticing she moved a little slower than usual. She may be miles better, but she was still healing.

He didn't speak until he unlocked his own door and stepped inside the apartment.

"You should be home resting."

"I need the exercise." She spoke absently, looking around the space.

It occurred to him she'd never seen where he lived before, but then again, she never had a reason to visit him. Her showing up at his doorstep had been a forbidden fantasy he never allowed himself to entertain.

"What can I do for you?"

She ended her brief inspection of his place and pulled a burgundy-colored folder from her handbag.

"My boss had one of the ADA's begin a file on you in preparation for"—she paused and then continued meekly—"charging you with Jason's murder. Under the new circumstances, they returned the file to me, but I thought you should have it."

She held it out to him, and he hesitantly took it.

"Thanks."

She smiled. "I wanted you to know it was all over. You can get on with your life now."

He nodded, tossed the folder on a small table by the door, and then went into the kitchen to grab a bottle of water from the refrigerator. He made another gesture to one of the barstools at the counter.

"Sit down," he said. "I'm glad you came by, because we need to talk. Something to drink?"

"No, thank you," she said, taking a seat at the counter.

He uncapped the bottle of water, took several gulps, and then tossed it into the trash. Then he eyed her and forced himself not to erupt but allow her to explain.

"I want you to be honest with me, Sophie. You think you can do that?"

"Of course."

He spoke slow and deliberate. "Have you been calling and texting me for the past year asking about Jason? I just want the truth."

She stared at him, speechless, and then tried laughing it off, but it came out sounding hollow and uncertain. "What are you talking about?"

He didn't know if it was her deliberate attempt to outright lie to his face or the fact that after weeks of not seeing her, she was still determined to play games. But whatever it was made him break his promise to himself to keep calm. He moved so fast, rounding the counter, she barely had enough time to jump from her barstool before he flung it away. It crashed onto the hardwood floor and rolled away, but he kept coming, until he was backing her up against the wall with his hands gripping her arms.

"Who are you? Tell me, goddammit, which one are you?"

"Ethan—"

"Which one are you?"

"Sophie! I'm Sophie. What the hell is wrong with you?"

He tightened his grip. "Prove it, and don't fucking tell me to look at your driver's license either. You could've swapped it with her."

She shook her head. "I— I— The tattoo! Angie has a tattoo on her shoulder, remember? I never got one."

"Tattoos can be removed. Try again."

"Ethan, stop it! You know it's me."

"No, I don't. I'm convinced the two of you have been playing games with me, and everyone you've ever met your entire lives. You're pros at it, so don't stand there and tell me I know it's you. I want you to prove it to me."

He could see the desperation and shock in her brown

eyes as she searched her memory for something that would satisfy him. Something that Angela never knew or could never impersonate.

"My scar," she said. "It's faint now, but it's still there."

He stared at her for a moment longer, looking for any sign of deception before slowly turning her around and lifting the back of her shirt. On the left side where her lower back met her waistline was the faint scar caused by him. Unable to resist, he slowly traced it with his forefinger, just like he did the night they made love. It was the only evidence he had that told him this was Sophie.

"I ended up needing stitches after all," she said. "That's the reason there's even a scar left."

Ethan turned her back around to face him. "A few weeks ago, Noah gave me the file Hailey had to investigate me. I found out there are over sixty calls, texts, and emails between you and me in a six-month period, and that I only called Angela two or three times. I've been going over it in my head, trying to understand how that can happen, and I only see one possibility. I want you tell me how that can happen. Give me any other reason than the one I'm thinking right now."

Her eyes grew wide by the time he was finished talking, but she kept her mouth shut tight.

"You were pretending to be her. The first time you called me to set up a date for drinks, you were pretending to be Angela, and I saved your number under her name."

"Ethan—"

"All the texts, emails, phone calls—it was you the whole time."

"Ethan please."

"Answer the question!"

"Yes."

"The first night we met for drinks?"

"Yes, it was me."

He slowly turned toward the mantle and looked at the picture. She followed his gaze, and when he turned back to her, both surprise and shame covered her features.

"That's you," he said. "Something told me it was always you."

She shook her head in confusion. "I…I never knew you had it framed."

Silence reigned for a long time as Ethan regarded her and thought back to every conversation they'd had. How could he not have known? He'd been so in love with this woman for so long, so how could he not have known it was her sitting beside him in that restaurant or her on the other end of the line this entire time?

Sophie hesitantly made her way to the couch and sat down. "Angie came to me saying she had a source naming you as Jason's murderer, but she needed a way to prove it. She thought that since you knew the two of us from childhood, you'd be more trusting and open up to her."

"When did you two switch places?"

"We never did. I only pretended to be her, but she never knew what I'd done. We took a ferry to Sausalito one day, and that's when she told me she planned to meet with you for drinks one night to catch up."

"Why did you take her place?"

"Because if there was even the slightest chance this source was telling the truth, I wanted to hear it from you myself. Angie had to fly back to L.A. and was going to cancel your meeting. When she went to the bathroom, I went into her phone, got your number and deleted your messages and your number from her contacts. Then I contacted you from my phone, pretending to be her and telling you I got a new number."

He stared, disbelieving, and then moved to sit in an armchair facing the sofa and leaned forward, resting his elbows on his knees. "Jesus, Sophie. So, one night turned into nearly three months?"

"I'm sorry. After a while, I was convinced you had nothing to do with it, so I began leaking rumors that Angela was working on a story involving you and the SFPD. I knew eventually it would get around to you, that you'd stop talking to me."

"To Angela," he corrected.

"Yes. But then you came to see me that afternoon at my office, and you were so angry. I tried so hard to keep you and Angie separated, but I didn't know you would follow her."

He remembered the no contact rule she'd insisted on when they first started talking. Now, he could see it was all a ploy to keep him from talking to the *real* Angela.

"I was at my wit's end. I went to her hotel room for answers. She seemed surprised to see me, and even said, she'd been trying to reach me. After I confronted her about what I'd heard, she got this strange look as if she'd realized something. After that, she told me to leave."

"She figured out what I'd done," Sophie said. "She sent me a text, telling me she knew."

Ethan shook his head. "All these fucking games. All this trouble. Why didn't you just ask me? Why didn't you just stay Sophie?"

She rose from the sofa and threw up her arms in exasperation. "If I stayed Sophie, you never would've confided in me. You always opened up to her, but never me. I admit I began to enjoy our conversations, even though I knew I was deceiving you. But I couldn't stop it."

"Why?" he asked, his voice filling with anger. "Why didn't you just ask me? Because you were afraid I would've admitted to killing him?"

"Yes!"

They fell silent again, and it was apparent they were both surprised by her admission.

"I suddenly didn't want to know anything," she said. "I was in way over my head. I just wanted to leave it all in the past. Jason was dead, and I didn't want you to be his killer. So that last phone call with me, I told you to stop talking. You were right. The night Angie was killed, I searched her hotel room for the story to get rid of it. I didn't want to know the truth anymore."

Without warning, she grabbed her handbag and headed for the door. "I should go. I'm sorry for everything I put you through. I'm sorry for all of it."

"Do you think I was in love with your sister?"

She had the front door open, but paused at his words and then turned back to face him. "A man confides in a woman who has his heart."

She started to walk out, but in the next instant, Ethan jumped up. There was no way in hell he was going to let her get away with that remark. He made it to the door in two steps and gripped one of her arms to pull her inside and kick the door shut behind them. Then he pinned her against the door with his hands tightening around her shoulders.

"Is that what you think?" he asked, his face so close she couldn't even try to look away.

"Let me go," she said, pushing against him.

"Answer me! Is that what you've been thinking this whole time? That it was her I wanted, because I shared things with her?"

"It doesn't matter now," she said. "They're all dead. Jason, Angie, Vanessa, Carl, and little Matthew. You know that there's nothing we can do to change that."

He took hold of her chin and bore his eyes into hers. "But we're not dead, Sophie. It's just you and me here, now, and we can move forward. Together."

The beautiful coffee tone drained from her face as she listened to his words. "I said let me go."

He pressed her harder against the door, his frustration with her now boiling over. "Damn you! I only confided in her, because she was a comfort to talk to, and I was ashamed to come to you. You were so kind, innocent, beautiful that I couldn't believe you wanted to be with me. I never wanted to come to you with my secrets, and the pain I felt when I talked about my dad, because I never wanted you to turn away from me."

"Then you were stupid, and didn't know me at all," she shouted. "I loved everything about you. Why couldn't you just trust me?"

"What good would it have done?" he asked, his voice rising to match hers. "You broke it off with me at the end of the summer. You ended things between us without any explanation and then turn up years later married to someone else. What good would it have done to confide in a woman who only wanted a summer fling?"

Just that quickly, her tone lowered and softened. "That's not true, Ethan."

She was staring up at him now, her eyes pleading with him to not believe the worst about her, and even in his haze of fury she looked so damned beautiful to him. He released her suddenly and pointed in the general direction of the mantle where the framed photograph of the two of them rested.

"You want to leave? Go ahead. You want to forget the past, take that fucking picture with you. I don't want any more reminders of how I played the damn fool for you."

"I won't take it," she said.

He stalked toward the mantle, snatched the picture from it, but she was there trying to take it from him and put it back.

"Ethan, don't. Keep it, please."

"I said I don't want it."

"Yes, you do. You're angry with me and have every right to be."

"Let go of the picture."

"I know I messed up," she said, "but don't shut me out now."

"Sophie, let go!"

The sound of glass shattering halted them both as the frame fell from their grasp and crashed to the floor. Ethan shook his head at the mess and then went to his hall closet, grabbed a dustpan and broom, and returned to see Sophie on her knees, carefully picking up the glass shards.

"Move out of the way and let me sweep it up," he ordered.

She continued picking up the pieces of glass, her head bent low.

"Sophie."

That's when he saw drops of tears fall to her hands, and something in him shattered as quickly as the glass frame. He put the broom and dustpan aside and knelt down to take the broken pieces from her hands. He carefully set them down and gently lifted her by the shoulders.

"I'm sorry, Ethan. In my heart, I knew you didn't kill Jason, but I needed someone else to blame. I was feeling so much guilt because maybe if I just let him stay and tried to work it out with him, he would still be alive. But I was humiliated, and I wasn't in love with him. So, I threw it all away."

She looked up at him, tears frozen in her eyes. "I fell in love with you that summer, but I threw you away, because I didn't want you to break my heart."

He stared at her, silently urging her to continue.

"Jason was right. We married each other for status. There was never any love between us. Not the kind that counts. But what I felt for you was real, and when I realized it never went away, that scared me."

He pulled her into his arms and buried his face in her hair. "All this time you've been trying to look out for me and not sure if you were protecting a monster."

He felt her hands move to his back and grasp him tightly. It felt so good, that he couldn't bear to let her go again. He placed his hands on the sides of her face and kissed each tear that stained her cheeks.

"Let me protect you for once," he said.

He took her by the hand and led her to his bedroom. Once he closed the door, he attacked her clothes, anxious to remove them and get to her soft skin. He tossed aside her bra and immediately put his mouth to one of her breasts.

Sophie moaned as she pulled down her jeans and kicked them to the side. Her panties followed next, and the moment he had her completely naked, he laid her down on the bed and climbed over her.

"You're still dressed," she breathed heavily.

He didn't answer but slowly spread her thighs and moved his head down to the center of her. He worshipped her there, licking, sucking, and kissing her most sensitive spot until she was screaming and calling for him and only him.

When he was satisfied she was completely his, he undressed, all the while watching her lying prone on his bed. When they finally came together, it was slow and deliberate. He could feel the relief sweeping over both of them. There were no more secrets, no more suspicions, and no more ghosts standing between them. Finally, he was free to love her openly without guilt or shame. Finally, Sophie was back in his arms.

* * *

Ethan unwrapped himself from Sophie and quietly climbed from the bed, careful not to wake her. He padded barefoot into the hall toward the kitchen for a drink of water and was stopped abruptly.

He swore viciously and looked down to see he'd stabbed himself with a piece of glass from the broken frame. In their rush to make love, he'd forgotten to sweep up. He pulled the piece of glass from his heel and gently set his foot back down. He bent over and pulled the picture from the frame.

Who knew that something so small meant so much to her, that the idea of him not wanting this picture would finally force her to open up to him about her true feelings. Looking down at their smiling faces, his arms around her waist, pulling her near to him, he knew she was right. He'd been angry, frustrated beyond belief, but never intended to let her walk out of here with this picture. He went to one of the end tables beside the sofa and pulled open the drawer to place the picture in beside the black jewelry case with the bracelet.

Ethan smiled. Tomorrow, he would go make a copy of the picture, have them both framed, and give one to Sophie. As for the bracelet—maybe the next time when he gave it to her, she'd tell him he had the right girl.

July 4, 2002

Olivia Thompson's parents spoiled their only daughter. For as long as Sophie could remember, Olivia hosted the biggest Fourth of July parties the school had seen. To be invited, was to be one of the "popular." One of the "chosen." She was Angela's friend, which automatically merited Sophie an invitation. Still, even though high school was two years behind them, Olivia was still trying to hold onto her reign. No doubt, being a sophomore in a big University pond, made the little fish feel small. But Sophie always enjoyed herself, because she loved Fourth of July, which came with the smell of barbecue, late evening, and of course, fireworks.

But this year, she wasn't going to enjoy any of it, because she was leaving the party just as soon as she arrived.

The party as a whole was lame: the food tasted bad, the music wasn't her style, all the guys were being jerks, and...

And Ethan was already there with someone else. Who was she kidding? Of course, he would latch on to one of the older girls. He'd graduated college this past spring and she was just entering her sophomore year. It was a miracle he was even attending Olivia's party, but then again, this was where all of his high school buddies were.

For the occasion, Sophie had dressed in her favorite jeans and flowy top, added a little makeup, and let her hair air-dry so it looked tousled and wavy—all to impress him. Angela commented on how pretty she looked. Then, she followed it up with a curious look, no doubt wondering who her twin was getting dolled up for.

But it had been all for nothing, because as soon as Sophie saw him hugged-up on a girl from his high school graduating class, she faked a headache and got out of there.

Olivia's house was a few miles from hers and their dad offered to drive them, but both girls refused and instead rode their bikes. Sophie was glad of that, too. The last thing she wanted to do was call her dad or Cynthia to pick her up because she was feeling broken-hearted.

On the solitary ride home, she wondered at what point she stopped seeing Ethan as the boy who lived two houses down from them or as the boy who worked odd jobs for her father, and started seeing him as a young man she had this ridiculous crush on. It was as if overnight she began to actually notice him, became crazy in love with him and hoped to God he felt the same way about her.

She crossed the street without paying attention, too caught up in school-girl fantasies. The car horn blared and immediately swerved out of the way. Sophie swerved too, but overestimated and fell to the side, landing on her back.

The car door opened and slammed shut. "Jesus Christ, Sophie! Are you all right?"

She instantly recognized the voice as the object of her fantasies and mortification swept over her.

"I'm fine," she groaned, trying to sit up.

"Let me help you," Ethan said, gently taking her elbow. "Where are you hurt?"

She nearly said she wasn't hurt, but as he tried to stand her up, she winced from something stinging her lower back.

"Will you check my back? It feels like something cut me."

He slowly inched up her top and the next thing she heard was a muttered curse.

"What is it?"

"Let me help you get in the car. I'll take you home. Do you have a first aid kit there?"

She nodded and let him lead her to the passenger side of his car. She noticed the girl he was with at the party wasn't there. Maybe they'd made plans to meet up somewhere later. When she was situated in the front seat, Ethan got her bike, put it in his trunk, and got inside the car. He sped the remaining few miles to her house without a word.

When they got to her house, she was surprised to see her father's car gone.

"Where are your father and stepmother?" he asked when they entered the front door.

She shrugged. "I guess they went out to see fireworks. There's a first-aid kit upstairs in the bathroom."

He followed her up the stairs and once inside the bathroom, he opened the first-aid kit and then looked at her strangely.

"What?" she asked.

"Do you feel comfortable taking off your top? I want to clean that wound."

She could have told him it was all she's ever dreamed about since he left for college four years ago. But instead of seeming too eager, she shyly nodded her head and slowly pulled off her top. Underneath her favorite top, she was wearing her favorite lace bra, but this wasn't how she expected Ethan to see her in it. However, when her top was off, he simply turned her around and began washing her lower back with soap and water.

"There must have been glass on the street and you scraped against it when you fell. Hopefully, you won't need stitches."

God, he was so close. He was actually touching her but seemed so oblivious to the torture he was putting her through. After cleaning the wound, he applied alcohol and some bandages and then finally handed her shirt back to her. Sophie slipped it on and then looked up at him.

"Thank you. I'm sorry I went out into the street like that."

He waved her apology off and then grabbed his car keys off the sink. "I'd better get going, Keep an eye on that bandage."

He turned preparing to leave.

"Ethan."

He stopped and looked at her expectantly. She knew she would never forgive herself if she didn't make this move. Without thinking, she took his face between her hands and kissed him. It only lasted a few seconds, because Ethan pulled away and stepped back. The sting of rejection stabbed at Sophie. Maybe he really did see her as just a little sister. Maybe he wasn't even interested in dating black girls. After all, she'd never seen him dating anyone but blondes and brunettes. She lowered her head in shame and complete embarrassment, praying he'd leave quickly and silently.

But in the next moment, she felt his hand snake around her neck, and he brought her to him for a kiss that was so deep, passionate, and enough to send her ego soaring. They kissed long and slow, getting to know one another in the most intimate way. It was frightening, but still new and exciting—something like summer love.

* * *

Afterward, they were lying on her bedroom floor huddled underneath blankets. Sophie kept looking up at him and knew she was wearing this silly grin on her face.

Ethan smiled back, turned his body toward her, and tucked one arm underneath the pillow.

"What's so funny?" he asked.

"I didn't think you liked me," she said. "I didn't even think you noticed me beyond Angie's twin sister."

"I noticed. I've always liked you. But, you were a good girl and out of respect for your dad, I left you alone."

"And now?" she asked.

"Now," he said, pausing to tuck a strand of her hair behind her ear, "we're both over eighteen, and this is the first time we've ever been alone without your parents, my mother or your sister around. I'm glad you kissed me."

He leaned forward and put his lips to hers. She didn't know what to do with her own hands, so she just put them on his firm waist and allowed him to take the lead. She moved her lips and tongue in response to his rhythm and reveled in the sensations coursing through her body, all the while celebrating the realization that this was Ethan kissing her.

When he pulled away, she lowered her head and spoke softly. "I thought you were seeing someone else. I saw you at the party—"

"So you were there," he said. "I thought I saw you. You left right away, didn't you?"

"I recognized her from school," she continued. "Didn't she graduate with you?"

"Jenna," he said, nodding. "Yeah we graduated together, and she's not my girlfriend. If you had stuck around a little longer before running away, you would have seen she was slightly buzzed and me handing her off to one of her friends to take her home."

"Oh." Sophie felt another wave of embarrassment sweeping over her.

"Are you staying here for the summer?" he asked, changing the subject and helping her maintain some of her dignity.

"Yes. Once I told my dad I wanted to go to law school, he wanted me to start looking for firms that would let me do summer work, but I talked him into letting me have one summer to myself. What about you? You graduated. What's next?"

"The police academy."

Sophie widened her eyes in surprise. "You want to be a cop?"

"Yeah, I decided halfway through my degree."

She nodded, impressed and surprised by the feeling of sadness that came over her. Would he stay in California or move to another state and begin his life? Would this be the only time she had with him?

Ethan took her hand and intertwined their fingers together. "I want to see you again, Sophie. I want to spend time with you this summer. Can we do that?"

* * *

"He said he wanted to see you? What did you say?"

Later that evening, Sophie was curled up in bed with the biggest smile on her face, watching Angela paint her toenails royal blue.

"I said sure."

"Sure?" Angela asked with a frown. "That's all you said?"

Sophie shrugged, knowing that wasn't all she'd said. She said, *I'd like that,* and they made love one more time before they both decided he should leave before her dad and stepmother returned home.

But as close as she and Angela were, she didn't want to tell her everything. She wanted so badly to keep something just between her and Ethan.

"So, you and Ethan?" Angela asked, her eyes focused on her task. "God, he's so hot. You'll have to switch places with me one night—"

"No," Sophie said sharply, the smile instantly melting from her lips.

Angela looked at her wide-eyed. "Wow. It was just a thought."

"I'm not switching, Angie."

"Okay, I get it. Veronica wants Archie all to herself. Greedy bitch."

Sophie smiled inwardly, because it was true. She did want Ethan all to herself. They'd played tricks on Ethan when they were younger, switching places and seeing how long it took for him to guess which one was which, but this was something entirely different. This, in Sophie's eyes, was something special.

Angela resumed painting her toenails. "Not to burst your bubble, but you know this is only for the summer."

"I know."

The thought had crossed her mind, but hearing Angela say it only confirmed that what she'd suspected was true. This summer was all she would have with Ethan.

"He just graduated college and probably has a girlfriend who's working some high-society internship this summer. He's just bored and wants to have a little fun with you before going into the police academy."

Sophie turned on her side away from her sister and faced the window.

"Don't worry about it," Angela continued. "Just have your fun."

"I will."

Sophie let it go and fell asleep with the promise that she was going to simply enjoy her first summer romance with Ethan and then end it when he went on to join the police academy and she returned to school in the fall. She was certain she'd never see him again, and all of this would eventually fade to somewhere deep and hidden in the back of her mind. Somewhere special and sacred—where all beautiful memories go.

* * *

Thank you for reading EXCHANGE! If you enjoyed Ethan and Sophie's exciting love story, you'll love the next book in the EX FILES series, EXPLOSIVE.

To save her life, Brian will help Carrie remember the past. But all he wants to do is forget the past—how much they loved each other, how they couldn't get enough of each other and how it all went so terribly wrong.

ONE-CLICK EXPLOSIVE NOW >
"Suspenseful, thrilling and entertaining."
"This book grips your heart and doesn't want to let go."

SIGN UP FOR LISA'S NEWSLETTER:
www.lisaryancampbell.com/newsletter

ABOUT THE AUTHOR

Award-winning Author, Lisa Ryan Campbell began writing as a small child using her mother's pink typewriting paper. Years later, she decided it was important to get a "real job" and attended Arizona State University to major in English with the goal of continuing on for both a Master's and Doctorate degrees in English and teach at the college level.

In 2002, Lisa graduated with a Bachelor's degree in English Literature and an Ancient Egyptian romance novel she wrote in her spare time. She decided then she would not be continuing on to graduate school, but instead joined Romance Writers of America and focused on her true love.

Lisa is an avid traveler and has seen many of the world's treasures in Egypt, Peru, Spain, France, Morocco, England, Mexico and the Caribbean. She spends her time mostly at her home in Colorado writing, reading and watching 1940's noir movies. She also loves to laugh, so you may frequently catch her watching reruns of Archer, Veep and The Office.

Sign up for Lisa's newsletter and find out more about her books at www.Lisaryancampbell.com and connect with her on social media.

www.ingramcontent.com/pod-product-compliance
Lightning Source LLC
Chambersburg PA
CBHW030401200726

48286CB00015B/2347